crooked as a dog's hind leg

ALSO BY TONI L. P. KELNER

FAMILY SKELETON MYSTERIES
(writing as Leigh Perry)

A Skeleton in the Family
The Skeleton Takes a Bow
The Skeleton Haunts a House

LAURA FLEMING MYSTERIES

Down Home Murder*
Dead Ringer*
Trouble Looking for a
Place to Happen*
Country Comes to Town*

Tight as a Tick*
Death of a Damn Yankee*
Mad as the Dickens*
Wed and Buried*

ANTHOLOGIES CO-EDITED
WITH CHARLAINE HARRIS

Many Bloody Returns
Wolfsbane and Mistletoe
Death's Excellent Vacation
Home Improvement: Undead Edition
An Apple for the Creature
Games Creatures Play
Dead But Not Forgotten: Stories from the World of Sookie Stackhouse

"WHERE ARE THEY NOW?" SERIES

Curse of the Kissing Cousins*
(originally published as Without Mercy)
Who Killed the Pinup Queen?*
Blast from the Past*

*available as a Jabberwocky ebook

crooked as a dog's hind leg

a laura fleming collection

toni l. p. kelner

jabberwocky literary agency, inc.

Publication History:

"Gift of the Murderer"
Originally published in *Murder Under the Tree*
Kensington Books, November 1993

"Marley's Ghost"
Originally published in *Murder Most Merry*
Kensington Books, November 1994

"The Death of Erik the Redneck"
Originally published in *Malice Domestic 5*, presented by Phyllis A. Whitney
Pocket Books, May 1996
Nominated for an Agatha Award

"An Unmentionable Crime"
Originally published in *Magnolias and Mayhem*, edited by Jeffrey Marks
Silver Dagger, January 2000

"Bible Belt"
Originally published in *Ellery Queen Mystery Magazine*, June 2002
Nominated for Anthony and Macavity Awards

"Old Dog Days"
Originally published in *A Hot and Sultry Night for Crime*, edited by
Jeffery Deaver
Berkley Prime Crime, February 2003

"Lying-in-the-Road Death"
Originally published in *Undertow: Crime Stories by New England Writers*
edited by Skye Alexander, Kate Flora, and Susan Oleksiw
Level Best Books, May 2006

To Dina Wilner
Best. Fan. Ever.

Contents

Welcome Back to Byerly!

The seven stories in this collection are all associated with the novels in my Laura Fleming mystery series. Two were written from the perspective of Laura herself, while the others featured other characters and settings from the books. They appeared in various anthologies and magazines, and have been out of print for years, so I'm happy to collect them for the first time.

In reading them, please bear in mind that they were written some years back. If you're wondering why the characters don't whip out their cell phones, it's because they were rarely seen back in the day. Social attitudes have shifted too, faster than I would ever have predicted. I considered updating the stories, but decided they work better set in their own little time capsules.

Gift of the Murderer

This story takes place in the time gap between the first two Laura Fleming novels: Down Home Murder *and* Dead Ringer.

I was glad I had saved Liz's present for last. Maybe it would help make up for Mrs. Hamilton's earlier abuse. "I believe this is for you," I said, handing her the glittery gift bag.

"For me?" she said, looking pleased. "Who did this come from?"

"A good elf never tells," I said solemnly. "Union rules."

She smiled and opened the bag. I could see my cousin Clifford watching from where he was playing Christmas carols on his guitar. The present was from him, but he was too shy to want Liz to know that. Liz reached into the bag and pulled out a long knife, the blade smeared with something dark.

"What on earth?" she asked.

"I don't know." I looked over at Clifford, but he seemed as confused as I was. "I think there's been some kind of a mistake," I said, but was interrupted by a shriek from a few feet away.

2 *crooked as a dog's hind leg*

Mrs. Hamilton had keeled over in her wheelchair, and one of the other residents pointed at her and shrieked again.

Liz dropped the knife back into the bag and thrust it toward me so she could run to Mrs. Hamilton. I was only a few steps behind her, though I didn't know that there was anything I would be able to do.

Liz put her hand on Mrs. Hamilton's back as if to straighten her up and then jerked her hand away. I was the only one close enough to see that her hand was covered in blood. A hole through the canvas back of the wheelchair matched the old woman's bloody wound.

I think Liz and I realized at the same instant that the smears on that knife had to be blood, which meant that I was carrying the weapon that had been used on Mrs. Hamilton.

I'll admit that I didn't have much Christmas spirit when my husband Richard and I came home to Byerly. My grandfather had been gone less than a year, and I wasn't sure that I wanted to celebrate without him. Still, I was trying to get into a holiday mood and had even agreed to help my cousin Vasti throw a party at the old folk's home a few days before Christmas. The last thing I expected was to end up investigating a stabbing.

Of course, if I had had one lick of sense, I would have called Vasti and canceled when the storm started that afternoon. But no, I let Richard talk me into going out in the middle of the worst ice storm to hit the mountains of North Carolina in years. It took us twenty minutes to chip out the car, and the roads were coated with ice.

I held just as tight as I could to the arm rest the entire time we were driving and tried my darnedest not to back-seat drive. Finally I couldn't help but say, "There's a stop sign just around that curve. You might want to start slowing down."

"Yes, dear," Richard said.

"Sorry. It's just that driving in this mess makes me nervous."

"Hey, I live in Massachusetts. No puny North Carolina winter can scare me."

After several years up North, I should have been used to winter weather, too, but I wasn't. "Of course in Boston they have snow plows to keep the roads clear," I reasoned. "And driving in ice isn't anything like driving in snow."

"Yes, dear."

"Sorry," I said again. I managed to stay quiet for another couple of minutes, but then said, "Take your time. We've got half an hour before we're due at the old folks' home."

"Isn't it supposed to be 'nursing home?' Or maybe these days it's a senior citizens' center."

"You're probably right." I felt the car slide, and gritted my teeth. Normally nothing in Byerly was more than ten minutes away from anything else, but we had already been on the road for twenty minutes and we weren't there yet.

"You're just afraid we're going to get into an accident and you'll have to go to the hospital dressed like that," Richard said with a grin.

I pulled down the sun visor on my side, looked into the mirror on the back side, and made a face at myself. "Do I look as foolish as I feel?"

"'The little foolery that wise men have makes a great show.' *As You Like It*, Act I, scene 1," he replied.

"Thanks loads. That makes me feel much better." Thanks to Vasti, I was dressed in green tights and a red garment that Richard said was a jerkin. My coat covered most of the outfit, but not the shoes and hat. The bells on the curled toes of my red slippers jingled every time I moved, and the plume on the Robin Hood hat constantly fluttered in and out of the corner of my sight.

"I think you look adorable," Richard added. "Just what I'd like to find in my Christmas stocking. Except that an elf shouldn't be frowning. Maybe we should have a little elf practice so you can learn to go hee hee and ho ho and important stuff like that."

I looked at him accusingly. "You're enjoying this, aren't you?"

He grinned.

"Keep it up," I said. "I'll tell the other members of your department that Boston College's Shakespeare specialist has been quoting from *Rudolph the Red–Nosed Reindeer*."

"Such cruelty," he said, shaking his head. "And so close to Christmas, too. You're liable to get coal in your stocking instead of that new software you've been hinting about. Just think of how happy those senior citizens are going to be when you and the others show up."

"They're going to laugh their fool heads off at us," I grumbled.

"You don't want to spoil the party, now do you? Remember, what the Bard said. 'A woeful hostess brooks not merry guests.' *The Rape of Lucrece*."

"Vasti's the hostess, not me. I'm just an elf."

"Well, if you didn't want to be an elf, you shouldn't have volunteered."

"I *didn't* volunteer," I protested. "Vasti volunteered me."
Vasti had originally arranged for four cousins to be elves at
the Christmas party she was throwing at the Byerly Nursing
Home, but when our pretty cousin Ilene got a better offer
and backed out, Vasti was left one elf short.

To be fair to Vasti, I hadn't fought her too hard when she
suggested I take Ilene's place. I was hoping that the party
would inspire at least a little of the Christmas spirit I was
missing this year.

I shoved the feather on that darned hat back into place
and looked at Richard in his blue jeans and Shakespeare
sweatshirt more than a little resentfully. "Vasti could probably come up with a costume for you."

"No, thanks," he said. "I don't look as good in tights as
you do."

Finally I saw the sign for the nursing home. "There it is.
Go right just after that post," I said, and was glad when we
managed to turn past the post and not into it. Not surpris-
ingly, there weren't many cars in the parking lot. Most folks
had enough sense to stay home on a night like this.

Still, the place looked like it was ready for a Christmas
party. Colored lights outlined the entrance, and there was
a wreath in every window. I recognized Vasti's style. As far
as she's concerned, if it's worth doing, then it's worth over-
doing.

With Richard and me helping each other across the
parking lot, we just barely kept from falling on our behinds.
Vasti was pacing across the lobby just inside the front door. I
guessed that as the hostess of this shindig, she rated a higher
rank than I did. Instead of an elf suit, she was dressed in a
red velvet dress with white fur around the sleeves and col-

lar, and had a perky Santa hat on top of her brown curls.
I would have thought boots would fit the costume better
than red patent-leather pumps, but Vasti always did have a
weakness for high heels.

"It's about time!" she said when she saw us. "I didn't
think y'all would *ever* get here."

"You said seven o'clock," I said, checking my watch. "It's
only a quarter til now." I thought that was pretty good, con-
sidering the ice storm.

"Seven? Laurie Anne, I know I said six–thirty. The triplets are late, too."

I thought about arguing with her, but decided it wasn't
worth the effort. "Well, we're here now."

"You can leave your coats in the closet behind the recep-
tion desk," she said, "and then come on down to the recreation room." She tapped her foot while we hung up our
coats, and then led the way.

About halfway down the hallway, she stopped to let
Richard and me pass her.

"What's the matter?" I asked, stopping too.

"Oh nothing," she said, and started up again. "I guess I
should have gotten you a bigger elf suit."

I followed her as best I could while trying to catch my
reflection in every shiny surface we passed. "It doesn't look
too tight to me," I said.

"Now don't you worry about it," Vasti said. "Most of
these old geezers can't see far enough to notice figure flaws."

What figure flaws? Maybe I wasn't Hollywood material,
but I didn't think I looked *that* bad.

By now we had reached the recreation room. I had to
admit that whoever Vasti had talked into doing the work

had done an wonderful job of turning the institutional room into a place where you didn't mind having a party. Tinsel garland and electric candles were scattered all around the room, and each of the tables circling the room had a silk poinsettia centerpiece.

There was an enormous Christmas tree in the center of the room, decorated with lots of blinking lights and shiny balls. A long table filled with platters of party food lined one wall, with punch bowls on either end. There was a small platform in one corner with music stands.

"Did I tell you that Clifford is coming to play Christmas carols?" Vasti asked.

"That's a great idea."

"I was just going to play tapes, but he said he wanted to come." She lowered her voice to what she thought was a conspiratorial whisper and said, "Don't tell him I told you, but I hear he's sweet on Liz Sanderson, one of the nurses here. I think she's Hoyle Sanderson's little sister. You remember Hoyle, don't you? Now he's blond but she's a redhead, so I can't decide if it's natural or not."

"Is Clifford serious about her?"

"Oh he's serious enough, but he's too doggone shy to tell her that. I don't know what on earth he's afraid of."

I did. I had been painfully shy in high school and through a good part of college. Clifford was afraid he'd be laughed at, just like I had been.

Vasti went on, "I've got half a mind to tell Liz that he's got a crush on her just to get it over with. Then maybe he'll quit mooning over her."

"Vasti, don't you dare."

"Why not? The worst that could happen is that she'd tell

me that she's not interested and ask me to break it to him gently."

The problem was, Vasti had never broken anything to anyone gently in her whole life. "Vasti," I started, but then reconsidered. If I left it alone, she'd likely forget about it anyway. Instead I said, "What do you want us to do? Everything looks pretty well set up already."

She picked a clipboard up off of a table and made a big show of looking at it. "Laurie Anne, you can arrange those Secret Santa gifts under the tree so they look pretty." She pointed to several boxes filled with wrapped packages. "You and the other elves will be handing them out later."

"Isn't that Santa Claus's job?" I said.

"No, because Arthur and I are going to be mingling and making sure that everybody is having a good time."

"Where is Arthur anyway?" Richard asked.

"He had a City Council meeting. Civic leadership takes up so much of his time." She sighed theatrically, which would have been more effective if I didn't know how much she loved being the wife of a city councilman. "I just hope he can make it through the storm."

She consulted her clipboard again. "Richard, those boxes on the table have cookies in them. You can set them out on those platters. All right?"

"'I will be correspondent to command,'" he said. "*The Tempest*, Act I, scene 2."

She paused a minute before deciding that he had said yes, and then said, "Now y'all two get busy, and I'm going to find a phone to see if the triplets are coming or not."

As I reached for a package, she added, "Laurie Anne, you might better be careful about bending over. I don't know how much strain those tights can take." With that burst of Christmas cheer, she disappeared into the kitchen.

Being an adult, I didn't let her comments bother me. Well, I stuck my tongue out at her behind her back, but I did put the presents around the tree like she'd asked. Then I went to see how Richard was doing.

"Aren't you done yet?" I asked in what I thought was a fair imitation of Vasti's soprano. "What on earth are you waiting for?"

"I'm trying, but Vasti baked enough cookies for an army," he said.

"Heaven forbid!" I said. "Vasti doesn't bake. She must have got someone else to bake them for her." I looked inside one of the boxes. "See? I know those are Aunt Nora's double–butter cookies. She always decorates them so pretty, I'd recognize them anywhere." I reached for a particularly fetching reindeer and then paused.

"Richard," I said, "tell me the truth. Do I look heavy in this outfit?"

He stepped back and studied me from a couple of angles. "To quote the Bard," he said, and then gave a piercing wolf whistle.

"Richard! This is a hospital. Sort of, anyway." I looked around to make sure no nurses had run in to see what was the matter. "Thank you, love, but that's not the kind of answer I was expecting."

"I calls them like I sees them."

"And what play did that come from?"

"Who said anything about a play? That's what Shakespeare used to say to Mrs. Shakespeare."

"Oh yeah? Then why did he only leave her his second best bed in his will?"

Vasti's return interrupted our literary discussion. "The triplets didn't answer their phone, so I guess that they're on their way. Richard, are you planning to finish that today?"

Richard saluted. "Yes, Mrs. Claus. Sure thing, Mrs. Claus. Right away, Mrs. Claus." Even Vasti had to grin as Richard made a show of rushing around like a chicken with its head cut off.

Richard and I had just finished arranging refreshments to Vasti's satisfaction when Idelle, Odelle, and Carlelle arrived, with Clifford in tow. The triplets were dressed in elf costumes like mine, but Clifford had escaped Vasti's penchant for costume and was just wearing a nice red and white sweater with his blue jeans. All four of them were carrying more wrapped presents.

"It's about time," Vasti said. "The party starts in five minutes."

Actually, we still had twenty minutes left, but Idelle knows how useless it was to argue with Vasti as well as I do. "Sorry Vasti. We had to finish wrapping the last batch of presents after work, and the roads are just terrible."

Then the sisters noticed me and Richard, and, as if one, said, "Laurie Anne! Richard! We didn't know you were coming! Just let us hug your necks!"

Richard and I were immediately surrounded by hugging and kissing cousins, followed by less effusive but equally sincere greetings from Clifford.

"Doesn't Laurie Anne make a cute elf?" Idelle asked her sisters.

"I don't know how Richard is keeping his hands off of her," Odelle agreed.

Carlelle said, "He just needs a little encouragement. Vasti, where'd you hang the mistletoe?"

"I didn't think mistletoe would be appropriate at a party for senior citizens," Vasti said stiffly.

"That's all right," Idelle said. "We brought some." She dug into her pocketbook, produced a sprig tied with red ribbon, and held it up high over my head. "Richard, Laurie Anne needs a kiss."

"'The kiss you take is better than you give,'" said Richard, and kissed me soundly, much to the delight of the triplets. "*Troilus and Cressida*, Act III, scene 5."

"That's enough of that," Vasti said. "We've got work to do." She handed out assignments, and we went to work.

Richard and I were hanging the mistletoe when he whispered, "How am I supposed to tell the triplets apart when they're dressed alike?"

"Check their necklaces," I said. "Each one is wearing her initial." Actually, I was used to the triplets dressing identically most of the time, so this was no worse than usual. I did notice that while my outfit was nearly the same as what the sisters were wearing, their jerkins were a good three inches shorter than mine.

Vasti must have realized the same thing, because I heard her say, "I didn't realize your outfits were so short when I bought them."

All three of the sisters raised their eyebrows in innocent surprise, even though we all knew that Carlelle was an expert seamstress and that hemming those jerkins wouldn't have taken her any time at all.

"Short skirts won't do you much good around here," Vasti said with a sniff. "Even you three aren't desperate enough to chase after men old enough to be your grandfather."

"But there's always the doctors," Idelle said cheerfully.

"And the orderlies," Carlelle added.

"And maybe even male nurses," Odelle said.

"I see y'all have given this some thought," Vasti said. "*Some* of us are here out of the goodness of our hearts to spread some Christmas cheer."

Idelle made a rude noise. "Who do you think you're fooling, Vasti? Everybody knows that the only reason you put this party together is for publicity for Arthur. Showing off how civic-minded he is."

"Well, helping out a husband is better than trying to catch one," Vasti snapped.

I decided it was time for some peace on Earth. "As long as the old folks have a good time, it doesn't really matter why we're here, does it?"

"I suppose not," Idelle admitted.

"And speaking of old folks," Vasti had to add, "we better get a move on. Our guests will be here any time now."

I was arranging the packages the triplets had brought under the Christmas tree when Clifford came up behind me and touched my shoulder. He was carrying a silver gift bag with a cascade of curling green and red ribbons tied around the handle.

"Laurie Anne, you're going to be handing out the gifts, aren't you?"

"The triplets and I are," I said.

He held out the bag. "Could you add this one to the stack?"

"Sure." I didn't see a tag. "Who's it for?"

"It's for Liz Sanderson. She's a nurse here."

Knowing how shy he could be, I didn't say a word, just put the bag under the tree. He was still standing there when I turned back around.

"I thought it'd be nice if she got a Secret Santa gift, too. All the residents are getting them," he said.

"That's very thoughtful of you, Clifford."

"I just didn't want her to feel left out. She works real hard."

"I'm sure she does."

He nodded a few times rapidly, and then said, "I better go tune my guitar. Bye now." He walked away more quickly than was strictly called for.

Richard walked up while Clifford was escaping and asked, "What's the matter with him?"

"I think he doth protest too much," I misquoted, and explained what Clifford was up to.

"Ah, young love," Richard said. "Reminds me of my first Christmas gift to a girl."

"What was that?"

"A paperback copy of *Romeo and Juliet*, with photos from the Zeffirelli film. I hoped it would inspire the lovely Jennifer to imagine me as Leonard Whiting and herself as Olivia Hussey."

"Did it work?"

"Yes and no. She fell in love with Leonard Whiting."

"Her loss," I said, and gave him a consoling kiss before finishing up with the packages. "There," I said when done. "As pretty as a Christmas card."

"I'll say," said Richard with a grin.

"I meant the tree."

"Of course," he said innocently.

We wandered over to the refreshment table, but the triplets had everything under control. Vasti rushed by a time or two with clipboard in hand, but I couldn't figure out why since we had finished all the work.

"It's time," she finally wailed, "and Arthur isn't here yet. The secretary at City Hall said he left ages ago."

"He probably got held up by the storm," Odelle said.

"It was terrible driving over here," Carlelle added.

"Like driving on a sheet of glass," Idelle said.

"But we can't have a Christmas party without Santa Claus," Vasti protested. Then she looked at Richard. "Richard, do you suppose—?"

"No," Richard said. "For one, I'm not Santa Claus material." That was true enough. You didn't often see a lanky, brown-haired, beardless Santa. "And for another, you haven't got a spare red suit."

Vasti nodded, acknowledging defeat. "Oh well. The photographer from the *Byerly Gazette* probably won't make it either."

"Thank the Lord for small favors," I whispered to Richard. "I am not about to have my picture taken while wearing an elf suit." Especially not for publication in the local paper.

Vasti looked at her clipboard one last time and nodded decisively. "We may as well get this show on the road. Clifford, play 'Jingle Bells.' Richard, you can serve punch. Elves, y'all go stand around the tree. And smile everybody! It's Christmas."

We all obeyed, right down to the smiles. Like she said, it

was Christmas. The double doors on the end of the room opened, and the nursing home residents slowly started coming in. When I saw the happy expressions on their faces, I decided it had all been worth it. Driving in the storm, doing what Vasti said, even wearing the elf suit.

The last folks to come in were in wheelchairs, mostly pushed by nurses, and I looked to see if I could spot the young lady who had caught Clifford's eye. I knew her as soon as I saw her. She was by far the youngest nurse there, and no matter what Vasti said, her red hair looked natural to me. There was just a sprinkling of freckles over her nose, and she had a curvy little figure that would have looked a lot nicer in an elf suit than in that starched nurse's uniform.

"Cute, isn't she?" Odelle whispered.

"Not bad, if you like them young and pretty," Idelle said.

"Look at Clifford," Carlelle said with a giggle. "He looks like he's been struck by lightening."

Well, not quite, but pretty close. If Liz had looked in his direction, there was no way she could have mistaken his expression for anything other than unabashed adoration. Then he caught himself and concentrated on his guitar playing.

"Isn't love wonderful," Carlelle sighed.

"You should know," Idelle said. "You've been in love three times this week yourself."

Odelle said, "When she gets a look at that doctor, she might try for four."

The three of them moved to converge on an admittedly attractive doctor. Meanwhile, the residents were converging on the refreshment table, and I went to help Vasti dispense cookies and other goodies. Richard was doing a booming business filling glasses, and I could tell he was dispensing Shakespearean quotes alone with the punch.

Once the first flurry was over, I managed to edge over to where the lovely Liz was making sure a particularly frail–looking patient had everything she needed. Just to help out, of course, not because I was nosy.

"Are y'all having a good time?" I asked them both.

The older lady looked confused. "She wants to know if you're having a good time," Liz said in a much louder voice. The lady bobbed her head and nibbled on a cookie.

"Mrs. Good is a little hard of hearing," Liz explained to me, "but she really is enjoying herself. They all are. We really appreciate y'all coming over here."

"It's our pleasure," I said, and was glad to realize that I was telling the truth. "I'm Laura Fleming, by the way."

She clearly didn't recognize my name, so I sighed to myself and added, "Some people call me Laurie Anne." As a matter of fact, almost everyone in Byerly did, no matter how hard I tried to change their ways.

"That's right. You're the one who lives in Boston, aren't you?"

I nodded. "There aren't many secrets in Byerly."

She smiled. "No, there aren't. Besides, I know some of your cousins. Ilene and Vasti, of course. And Clifford."

Had I noticed a certain emphasis on that last name? "I think he mentioned you to me," I said nonchalantly.

"Did he?" she said, and she didn't sound a bit nonchalant. She looked over to where he was playing and singing "Christmas in Dixie." "He's got such a nice voice. Reminds me of Garth Brooks."

Yes, there was definitely attraction on both sides. Now, how would I get them under the mistletoe? Stop that, I told myself firmly. I was getting to be as bad as Vasti.

Speaking of Vasti, she was ready to speak for herself. She waved for Clifford to stop singing, and stood next to him. "Is everybody having a nice time?" she asked in a voice loud enough that even Mrs. Good would have no trouble hearing her. She waited for an affirmative murmur, and then said, "Well, we're all real glad. I do have some bad news for you, though. Santa Claus got stuck in the ice out there, and he's not going to be able to make it. But don't you worry! He sent some of his very favorite helpers with a whole bunch of presents for you folks. Y'all just stay where you're at, and they'll be coming around in a minute."

That sounded like a cue for us elves, so we met by the Christmas tree. Vasti and her clipboard joined us.

She said, "Now all of the packages are labeled, so you shouldn't have any problem handing them out."

I said, "How do we know who's who?"

"I sent around pins for everybody with their names on them a couple of days ago. They're *supposed* to be wearing them."

Now that she mentioned it, I saw that all of the residents were wearing red and green badges. Whatever faults Vasti might have, she did know how to arrange a party.

Vasti consulted her clipboard and asked the triplets, "Did y'all put together a list of what you got for people? I want to cross-reference it with my Secret Santa list."

"We didn't quite finish typing it up," Carlelle said in a tone that meant that they hadn't even started yet. "You don't need it right now, do you?"

"I suppose not," Vasti said. "Laurie Anne, you would not believe what some of these people asked for for Christmas." She rolled her eyes. "All kinds of candy when they know it's not good for them and frilly lingerie they don't need any more than the man in the moon. One old coot wanted dirty magazines. Now what good are dirty magazines going to do an old man?"

"Maybe looking is better than nothing," I said.

"And what if he gave himself a heart attack?" she asked indignantly. "How would I explain that? I told the triplets to just ignore any silly gift ideas like that."

The triplets nodded dutifully.

Vasti said, "Now you four get busy, and I'll go see how the refreshments are holding out." She clattered away.

"Did you three get stuck buying and wrapping *all* of the presents?" I asked. There were thirty or forty residents, and it looked like there was a gift for each of them under the tree.

"Well, most of them," Carlelle said. "Every patient is somebody else's Secret Santa, and those that are able did their own shopping. We just shopped for those who couldn't."

Idelle said, "You didn't think Vasti did any of it, did you?"

"I think she likes to organize things so she doesn't have to do any of the work herself," Odelle said.

"That's not fair," Carlelle protested. "She works hard telling everybody else what to do." The other triplets and I snickered, and she realized how that had sounded. "You know what I mean. Besides, we love shopping, don't we?"

Her sisters nodded.

"Laurie Anne, I'd love to come see you in Boston," Idelle said. "Christmas shopping must be so much fun with all those stores you have up there."

"To tell you the truth, Richard did most of our shopping this year. I just couldn't get into the mood," I said.

"Really?" Carlelle said. "I just love Christmas shopping. All the sales and the people and the Christmas music and all."

Most years I had felt the same. It's just that every time I went into a store this year, I kept seeing gifts that would have been perfect for Paw. And Paw wouldn't be here this Christmas.

"Anyway," I said, not wanting to pursue the subject, "we better get going before Vasti Claus sics the reindeer on us."

While we handed out gifts, Clifford led the residents in Christmas carols. If Liz noticed that he was watching her while he sang, she didn't show it directly. Still, she tended more to the residents who were close to the singing than to those who weren't.

Apparently the Secret Santas had done a good job choosing gifts. I heard right many ooh's and aah's. I had always heard that Christmas was for children, but you wouldn't know it from watching these people. They were having themselves a good old time.

I was on my way back to the tree to pick up another gift when I saw one man having troubles getting his package open. "Can I give you a hand with that, Mr. Biggers?" I said, after checking his name tag.

"That would be real nice," he said.

I pulled the paper off for him, broke the tape holding the box shut with my thumbnail, and then put it back on his lap so he could open it himself.

"Thank you kindly." He pulled the box top off, looked inside, and grinned like the cat who ate the canary. "My, my, my," was all he said.

I looked in to see what had him so pleased. The box was filled with copies of *Playboy* and *Penthouse*. Mr. Biggers turned a few pages and grinned even wider. "My, my, my."

I saw Vasti approaching, and I guess Mr. Biggers did, too, because he slid the lid back on top of the box.

"Did you get a nice present?" Vasti asked brightly.

"I sure did," he said. "Just what I wanted."

"Aren't you going to show it to me?" she said.

"Oh, this isn't anything you'd be interested in," he said, with a sideways look at me. "Just a bunch of sports magazines. I dearly love reading about a good game."

"Well, I hope you enjoy them." She clattered away.

Mr. Biggers winked at me and said, "Merry Christmas, young lady."

I wondered if the gift had been purchased by one of the triplets or all three in collusion. Even as children, there had been nothing they enjoyed half as much as putting one over on Vasti. No wonder they hadn't made her a list.

Encouraged by my success in spreading Christmas cheer, I looked around to see if there was anyone else I could speak to. I saw a wheelchair–bound woman off in a corner by herself. "Hello there Miz..." She wasn't wearing a name tag, and only looked at me balefully when I paused for her to insert her name. She probably never had been a very pretty woman, but with that expression, she was downright intimidating. My Aunt Maggie would have wanted to know how much she'd charge to haunt a house. "Hello there," I finally said. "Did you get a nice present?"

She mumbled something, and I realized that only the left side of her face was actually moving. The right side just sagged.

"I beg your pardon?" I said.

She grimaced and mumbled louder but I still couldn't understand. Fortunately another patient walked up with two cups of punch. His name tag said Frank Morgan.

"I'm afraid Mrs. Hamilton is a little hard to understand right now," he said. "Just give her another week in physical therapy, and she'll be quoting Shakespeare like that young fellow who was pouring the punch."

Mrs. Hamilton said something, and this time I caught enough of it to tell that it wasn't very nice.

Mr. Morgan winced, but just said, "Here's your punch, Sadie," and tried to hand it to her. Instead of taking the cup, she shoved it aside, knocking it out of Mr. Morgan's hand and splashing punch onto the floor.

"I'll go get something to wipe that up," I said, but Liz must have seen what had happened because she appeared with a paper towel.

"Accidents will happen," she said smoothly, and wiped it up. "Mrs. Hamilton, did you want another cup of punch?"

I swear I could see the blood rushing to Mrs. Hamilton's face. She struggled for a long moment with what she wanted to say before finally spitting out, "BITCH!"

There was a moment of silence, and I knew the whole room must have heard her. Liz went white, and I realized just how young she was. She was probably still in her early twenties, not nearly old enough to be able to take that without it hurting her feelings.

Mr. Morgan said, "Maybe I should take Sadie to visit

with the others." He started to push the wheelchair but had only gone a few steps when Mrs. Hamilton used her good arm to switch on the electric wheelchair and move away from his grasp. I saw rather than heard him sigh, and he followed along after her.

Everyone else in the room went back to what they had been doing, leaving me and Liz standing there.

"Are you all right?" I asked.

"I shouldn't let her upset me like that," she said, more to herself than to me. "She's old and she's real sick."

"I'm sure she didn't mean it."

"Actually she probably did," Liz said with a half smile. "Sadie Hamilton has been after me ever since I started working here, probably because she knows how young I am. The other nurses keep telling me that if I can put up with her, I can put up with anything."

"Is she that bad?"

"Any of the residents can get grumpy sometimes, but Mrs. Hamilton is just plain mean. She's been even worse the past few weeks. She had a stroke the day after Thanksgiving, and she pretty much lost the use of the right half of her body. She could probably get some of it back in physical therapy if she'd just try, but she won't. She just mumbles the most awful things at us when we try to show her. How can you help someone like that?"

"You can't," I said.

Liz nodded. "I know, but I have to keep trying." She spotted the punch glass on the floor and picked it up. "I better get back to work."

"Me, too," I said, and returned to my station at the Christmas tree to finish handing out presents. We were just about done when I saw the bag for Liz still sitting there. That's when I got the idea of giving it to her to cheer her up, and instead handed her the knife that had been used to stab Mrs. Hamilton.

∾❧∾

Liz had been trained well. Even after seeing the wound, she hesitated only a second before checking for a pulse.

"Is she...?" I asked.

"She's alive," Liz said, and then called out, "Get Dr. Buchanan!" Another nurse ran to comply.

"You better call the police, too," I told Liz in a quieter voice. Liz nodded, and I saw the doctor coming in at a run. I stood back out of the way while he and Liz exchanged a few words and then wheeled Mrs. Hamilton out of the room, still slumped over in the wheelchair.

I looked around for Richard. The other residents didn't seem as upset as I felt like they should be. After a slight pause, they kept on eating cake and drinking punch as if nothing had happened. Even the woman who had been shrieking had quieted down and was nodding in time with the carol Clifford was playing.

Of course, I told myself, they didn't know Mrs. Hamilton had been stabbed. As far as they knew, she had succumbed to another stroke or maybe a heart attack, and probably neither of those were unusual around here. Should I tell them? I couldn't think of a good reason why I should, at least until we knew more.

I finally spotted Richard coming out of the kitchen with a tray of cookies. I met him at the refreshment table and pulled him into a corner.

"What's the matter?" he asked as soon as he got a good look at me.

"Didn't you hear the scream?" When he shook his head, I told him what had happened.

As soon as I finished, he said, "Are you sure that's the knife that was used on her?"

"Of course I'm not sure," I snapped, "but I would hope that there aren't any other bloodstained knives floating around the place."

"Is there anything else in the bag?"

"I don't know." I pulled the bag open, but all I saw was the knife and some red tissue paper. "I don't want to touch anything." I looked around the room. "The awful thing is that whoever did it is probably still in here. I mean, we'd have noticed an outsider."

"I assume the police are on the way."

"I hope so. I told Liz to call, and I'm sure the doctor would want them here, too." We stayed there watching the party uneasily and listening for the siren which would mean that the police had arrived. Instead Liz came over to me.

"Laurie Anne? Chief Norton wants to talk to you." Richard nodded, and I followed her.

"Is she here?" I asked as we walked.

"No, she's on the phone." She led me to a paneled office marked Dr. Buchanan. "Chief Norton is on line 3." She closed the door behind her as she left.

I picked up the phone, and punched the blinking button. At first, all I heard were sirens and yells. "Junior?"

"Is that you, Laurie Anne?" she said, speaking loudly enough to be heard over the cacophony.

"It's me."

"Hold on just a minute, will you? I've got myself one hell of a mess to deal with out here. Three carloads of fools drinking beer ran into one another, and now they want to fight about whose fault it was."

That explained the noises I was hearing. I could just picture Junior in her blue jean jacket and cowboy boots wading into the middle of it. Even if she was only five foot three, she'd have them in order pretty quickly.

I've known Junior since we were five years old, and even then she wanted to follow in her father's footsteps as chief of the Byerly police department. Her name was the result of Andy Norton's wish for a son to name after himself. When his fifth daughter was born, he named her Junior. Naturally his sixth child was a boy. He became Andy Norton the Third, and Junior's deputy.

Junior finally came back to the phone. "Are you still there?"

"I'm here."

"Tell me, Laurie Anne. Why is it that every time you come to town, something like this happens? No, don't answer that. I don't have time. What's going on up there?"

I quickly told her what little I knew.

Junior said, "The doctor says that Mrs. Hamilton is going to make it, but it was damned close. Another inch or so, and she'd be gone. I hear you gave Liz Sanderson a gift bag with the knife that did the job."

"I think so."

"Where is it now?"

"I've got it." I hadn't known what else to do with it.

"Good. Don't let it out of your sight. Liz said there was no tag. Do you know who it was from?"

"Yes," I admitted reluctantly. "My cousin Clifford asked me to give it to her."

"Is that so?" she asked, and I just knew she had raised one eyebrow.

"Not the knife," I added hurriedly. "I was watching him when Liz pulled it out of the bag, and he was as surprised as she was. The bag wasn't sealed or anything, and it's been under the Christmas tree all evening. Anyone could have seen it and put the knife in."

"We'll see. What else was in the bag?"

"I haven't looked."

"I imagine you've got fingerprints all over the outside by now, so we won't worry about that, but don't put your hand inside. Just hold the bag by the bottom and spill out whatever's in there."

I cleared some papers off of the desk blotter, and then did as she instructed. The knife fell out first and was followed by two other items. "It's a Garth Brooks cassette tape, still sealed, and a little gold cardboard box. Like a gift box."

"See if you can use a pencil or something to open that box without touching it."

"I'll try." Fortunately Clifford hadn't taped it shut, and I used two paper clips to get it open. "It's a pair of gold earrings. Hoops." I leaned closer. "They aren't real gold, but they are pretty."

"Anything else in the box?"

I poked around with a pen. "Just cotton padding."

"How about in the bag?"

"Tissue paper."

I heard someone on Junior's end call her name, and Junior told me, "Hold on." A few minutes later she said,

"Now what kind of knife is it? And remember not to touch it."

To tell the truth, I wouldn't have touched it if she had asked me. "It looks like a regular kitchen knife. Wooden handle, used but not real old. It looks shinier along the point, like it's been sharpened."

"It would have to be right sharp to go through the wheel-chair and into Mrs. Hamilton's back."

"I suppose so."

I heard someone yelling for her again, and Junior must have dropped the phone she was talking on, because I heard it bounce off of something. Or someone.

This time she was gone longer, and I could hear her cursing long before she came back to the phone. "Laurie Anne, I've got a problem."

"Are you all right?"

"I am, but one of these fools just hit Trey upside the head and knocked him cold." Before I could ask, she added, "I'm sure he's going to be fine, but now I'm going to have to deliver this baby all by my lonesome."

"What baby?"

"I don't have time to talk about it right now, Laurie Anne. Is there a Bible anywhere around there?"

I didn't even ask, I just looked around the shelves. "I don't see one."

"Well, get a book, any book, and open it up."

I grabbed a Physician's Desk Reference.

"Put your left hand on the book and raise your right hand."

I did so, wondering what she was up to.

"Shoot, now how does it go?" Junior said. "Do you,

Laurie Anne Fleming swear to uphold the laws of Byerly, North Carolina, and the United States, not necessarily in that order. Say, 'I do.'"

I said, "I do."

"Then by the power invested in me as Chief of Police in Byerly, I hereby make you a deputy of the Byerly Police Department, with all the rights and responsibilities I decide to let you have. You can put your hand down now."

"Junior—"

"Laurie Anne, I wouldn't ask you if I didn't have to, but I don't have any idea of how long it's going to be before I can get there. I'd ask for someone from the county or the state to take over, but they're all tied up with the ice storm same as I am. Besides, you and I both know that you're going to be asking questions anyway, don't we?"

"Probably," I admitted. I was getting a reputation around Byerly for curiosity.

"That's what I figured. This way you're obliged to tell me everything you find out, not just the stuff that doesn't affect your family."

That smarted, but she was right. I had avoided giving Junior information in the past when I thought it might cause more harm than good. "I've always told you everything eventually, haven't I?"

"Yes, you have, and that's why I'm trusting you now. At the very least, I need you to make sure that whoever it was who tried to kill Mrs. Hamilton doesn't try again. If you find out anything else in the meantime, that's fine too. All right?"

I could think of a good dozen reasons why I should tell

her no, but of course what I said was, "All right, Junior." If she could deliver a baby in the middle of an ice storm, I could do this.

"Good. I'll be there when I can. Bye." She didn't wait for me to say goodbye back.

I hung up the phone and maneuvered the knife and Clifford's presents back into the gift bag while I tried to decide what I should do next. As Junior had said, the first priority was to protect Mrs. Hamilton. Obviously someone had to be with her at all times. The question was, who? What if I used the very person who wanted to kill her as a guard? Who could I trust?

Myself, of course, and Richard. And Vasti, and the triplets, and Clifford. Then I stopped. Junior was trusting me to be at least somewhat objective, and if they hadn't been my cousins, I wouldn't have crossed them off of the list so quickly. I had to be fair about it. I was going to assume that Richard was innocent no matter what, but that was as far as I could go without more proof. I could post Richard in Mrs. Hamilton's room, but I didn't think he'd be thrilled about my trying to find a murderer on my own. And actually, I wasn't too thrilled about the idea myself.

A knife in the back sounded like a solitary act to me, so maybe I could conclude that only one person was involved. If so, that meant that the solution was to use two guards at a time. That would have to do.

Liz was waiting for me outside the office, pacing nervously.

"Is Chief Norton on the way?" she asked.

"I'm afraid not. She's tied up because of the storm."

"Then what are we going to do?"

"Don't worry," I said, trying to sound a lot more confident than I felt. "She's deputized me temporarily."

She didn't look impressed, and I can't say that I blamed her. I don't know that I would have trusted a deputy in green tights myself.

"Where's Dr. Buchanan?" I asked. "I need to ask him some questions."

"He's in the infirmary."

"Can you show me the way?" She nodded, and I followed her.

I have never liked nursing homes. They smell too much like hospitals, and they're too quiet. Now that I knew that there was an attempted murderer on the loose, this place was downright creepy. I stuck close to Liz and watched all around as we walked.

The infirmary consisted of a treatment room and a small ward of half a dozen beds. One bed had been curtained off, and Dr. Buchanan had just closed the curtain behind him when we came in.

"Dr. Buchanan? My name is Laura Fleming. Chief Norton has deputized me to take charge here." I thought that the phrase "take charge" was properly official without promising too much. "I'd like to ask you some questions about Mrs. Hamilton's injury."

"Fine," he said, looking at his watch, "if you can ask them in a hurry."

"Are you going somewhere?" I asked, following him as he kept on moving. Liz trailed along behind me.

"I just got a call from the hospital in Hickory. I see patients there as well as looking after the residents here, and they need me tonight. There have been a number of weather–related incidents."

"What about Mrs. Hamilton?"

"She should be fine. The wound was deep, but no vital organs were hit, and there was relatively little loss of blood. We got to her before she could go into shock. The nurses will monitor her for complications, of course, but I don't foresee any difficulties."

"I see," I said, a little breathless from trying to keep up with him. "Could you slow down a little bit?"

"Sorry."

"Does what you said mean that this wasn't an attempted murder after all?"

"Oh, I wouldn't say that. Another inch and the knife would have hit her heart. I'd guess that the heart was the intended target, but the difficulty of stabbing through the wheelchair back deflected the aim."

"Does that imply that the person knew what he or she was doing?"

"Combat knowledge, you mean?"

"Or medical," I said. Liz didn't look happy at that suggestion.

Dr. Buchanan stopped a second to consider it. "In most groups of people that would be a reasonable assumption, but not here. You see, most of our residents spend a fair amount of time reading up on their bodily processes. Comes with growing old, I suspect. Most of the residents' library is made up of medical books of one kind or another. Anyone here could easily have researched the issue."

By now, we were at the front door and Dr. Buchanan was

pulling on an overcoat. He asked, "Was there anything else? I really need to get to the hospital."

At the moment I didn't have any other questions. I wasn't sure what Junior would say about my letting a possible suspect leave the scene of the crime, but I didn't think I had any right to stop him, under the circumstances. Besides, I was almost certain he had not been in the party for very long after the triplets made their play for him. The three of them together did tend to scare men off.

I said, "I guess not. Chief Norton will probably want to talk with you later on."

"Fine. I expect to be at the hospital for some time to come." He turned to Liz. "Let me know if there are any problems with Mrs. Hamilton or any of the others."

"Yes, doctor. Be careful out there."

I must admit I would have preferred for him to stay. A doctor made a comforting authority figure, and I wasn't too happy with assuming the role myself. "Who's officially in charge of the home now?" I asked Liz after he left.

"I'm not sure. Usually Mrs. Higgenbotham would be. She's the head nurse for the night shift. Only she couldn't make it in tonight because of the ice storm. And Mrs. Donahue, the administrator, left early for the same reason. As a matter of fact, we're on a skeleton shift because so many people stayed home. There's only six nurses, counting me, two orderlies, and the cook."

That kind of decided it for me. If I didn't take charge, no one would. I said, "The first thing we have to do is to make sure that Mrs. Hamilton is protected. Someone needs to be with her at all times."

"One of the nurses is in there now. I'll make sure she stays there."

"Good. I'll be sending one of my cousins to join her."

"What for?"

"Until we know who tried to kill Mrs. Hamilton, we can't trust anyone to be in there with her alone."

"Surely you don't think that one of us—"

I cut her off by holding up my hand the way Aunt Maggie always does. "I don't think anything yet. The point is that we have to protect Mrs. Hamilton the best we can. Is she conscious?"

"No, she's under sedation."

"Fine. If she should come to and say anything, I need to know at once. Come with me so you can show my cousin back to the infirmary." I walked briskly away, imitating Dr. Buchanan's walk and hoping that she would follow. Fortunately, she did.

The party was still going on, but clearly the news about Mrs. Hamilton had begun to spread. Instead of mingling, people had gathered into tight little knots around the room. I noticed that no one was going near the spot where Mrs. Hamilton had been stabbed.

Richard was standing with Vasti and my other cousins. What I really wanted was a few minutes alone with him, but I could tell from the expression on Vasti's face that I wasn't going to get it. As soon as she saw me, she put her hands firmly on her hips. "Where have you been? What is going on around here? Where's Junior? How am I supposed to throw a decent party when I don't know what's going on?"

If Dr. Buchanan leaving hadn't convinced me, that

would have. I couldn't afford to hesitate in taking charge, because if I did, Vasti was bound to leap into the vacuum. I might be unsure about my own skills, but I knew all too much about Vasti's.

As soon as she stopped to take a breath, I jumped in with, "Y'all must know what happened. Junior can't get through the ice storm, so she's put me in charge. Carlelle, Liz is going to take you to the infirmary to keep an eye on Mrs. Hamilton. There's a nurse there if she needs anything medical, but I want you to stay there and make sure no one bothers her. Don't leave her alone, not even to go to the bathroom, unless you get word from me."

The triplets looked at each other for a second, but after the silent conference, Carlelle nodded. "All right." She followed Liz away.

By now Vasti had her breath back. "Laurie Anne, just what in the Sam Hill is going on?"

I ignored her. "Idelle, I want you go outside and check the parking lot. There were only a few cars there when we got here, and they should all be covered in ice. See if there are any without ice, and if there are, get the license number. And see if you can tell if any cars have left."

"How is she going to do that?" Vasti wanted to know.

Idelle said, "I'll check to see if any of the parking spots aren't iced over yet, of course." She also left without questioning me.

"Laurie Anne," Vasti said, "are you saying that whoever it was might still be lurking around?"

Obviously I was, so I went on. "Richard, can I have your handkerchief?" He handed it to me, and I gingerly pulled the knife out of the gift bag I was still carrying. "Odelle, check the kitchen and see if there are any other knives like this around. I want to know if the knife came from here." She took a good look at the knife, nodded, and headed for the kitchen.

"Laurie Anne—" Vasti started, and I knew I was going to have to come up with something for her to do.

"Vasti, I want you to keep the party going. Don't let anybody leave the room, but don't scare them either. Get the nurses to help you if you need them." I touched her shoulder. "I'm counting on you to keep these folks calm."

Though she looked a little suspicious, she nodded and said, "All right, then. Why didn't you say so in the first place?" She started corralling nurses and residents.

"What about me?" Clifford said.

"I want you to come with me and Richard for a minute," I answered, and we went into a quiet corner where I could still see what was going on.

"Clifford," I said as gently as I could, "did you know that knife was in the gift bag?"

"Of course not! The first time I saw it was when Liz fished it out of the bag."

"I found a Garth Brooks tape and a pair of earrings in the bag, too. Is that what you meant for Liz to have?"

He nodded. "She's real fond of Garth Brooks."

"And that's all that was in that bag when you gave it to me?"

"That's all. Does she know it was from me? Liz, I mean?"

"Not yet," I said. He was so concerned about his crush being found out that he hadn't even realized that he was a suspect. "You heard what Mrs. Hamilton said to Liz, didn't you?"

"Everybody in this room heard it," he said indignantly.

"You must have been pretty angry at her. Feeling about Liz the way you do."

"You bet I was! I know she's old and all, but she's got no call to be talking to people like that. Especially not to Liz." He finally caught the implication. "Laurie Anne, you don't think I stabbed her, do you?"

"No, I don't," I said truthfully, "but I had to ask. That knife showing up in your gift right after Mrs. Hamilton was so mean to Liz does look funny."

"I guess it does," he admitted. "If it had been a healthy man who said those things, I probably would have started something, but I never would have with a sick old woman. And you know I would never have stabbed anybody in the back like that. Anyone could have stuck that knife in the gift bag. All kinds of people were all around the Christmas tree tonight."

"Did you see anyone in particular over there?" I asked hopefully.

He shook his head. "I wasn't really paying attention because Vasti had me playing carols."

"Did you see anyone over near Mrs. Hamilton? Before she collapsed, I mean?"

Again he shook his head. "I don't think so. People were coming and going so much, I don't know where anyone was." Then he added with a shy grin, "Except for maybe Liz."

"How long have you known Liz?"

This time he knew where I was leading. "Long enough to know that she'd never do anything like that. Ever since she was a little girl, she's been just as nice. She told me herself that the residents say ugly things to her all the time, but she knows that they don't really mean it."

"All right," I said. Asking him about Liz had been foolish anyway. He wouldn't have a crush on her if he thought she was that kind of a person. "Richard and I are going to see if we can find out who did this. In the meantime, I want you to help Vasti keep people calmed down. Play them some more Christmas music. Maybe that will help."

"All right," he said. He picked up his guitar, but then hesitated. "You believe me, don't you Laurie Anne?"

"Of course I do, Clifford," I said, and I guess he could tell I meant it. All right, I wasn't being objective, but I had changed Clifford's diapers. There wasn't a mean bone in that boy's body.

As soon as Clifford went, I hugged Richard. "I'm afraid we've been drafted. Or at least, I have. Are you game?"

"'I will be correspondent to command,'" he said. "*The Tempest*, Act I, scene 2."

"You used that one already today."

"Did I? 'Heaven lay not my transgression to my charge.' *King John*, Act I, scene 1. So where do we start?"

"With Mrs. Hamilton, I think. She's from Byerly, but I don't know a whole lot about her."

"Are you implying that you know about everyone else in Byerly?"

"Not everybody, of course, but most everybody. By their family if not any other way." I pointed to a bearded man in a red and green sweatshirt. "That's Mr. Honeywell. I went to school with his grandchildren, and he used to play Santa Claus at our Christmas party." Then I nodded at a skinny woman with jet black hair. "Mrs. Peabody has been dying her hair that color for as long as I can remember, but she always does it at home because she doesn't want anyone to know that it's not natural."

"I was completely fooled," Richard said dryly.

"Since I don't know Mrs. Hamilton, I guess our first step is to find out about her." Liz picked that moment to return.

"I left your cousin with Mrs. Hamilton," she said, "but I still don't think it's necessary."

"Maybe not," I conceded, "but better safe than sorry. Now, if you don't mind, I want to ask you some questions about Mrs. Hamilton." From out of the corner of my eye, I saw Clifford looking at us worriedly. "Maybe we could use Dr. Buchanan's office." I wasn't about to question Liz with Clifford watching me like that.

As soon as we got there, I waved Liz to one of the visitor chairs and took the desk chair myself. I thought I might as well try to look official. Richard picked up a pad of paper and a pen from the desk, and then pushed his chair back behind mine. Obviously he was going to let me run the show.

I took a deep breath. "I guess my first question is, do you know of any reason why anyone would want to kill Mrs. Hamilton?"

"No!" she said, and I guess she must have realized she answered a little bit too quickly. "I know you're thinking about what she said to me tonight, but believe you me, she's said the same and worse before. To all the nurses, not just to me."

"Does she just fuss at you nurses, or does she bother the other residents, too?"

"Oh she's like that with everybody: nurses, doctors, other residents, the kitchen staff, even other people's visitors."

"Does she not get visitors of her own?"

Liz shook her head. "Not since I've been here. She's got a couple of daughters who live in the state, but they never come to see her. They'll send a card once in a while, but that's about it."

No wonder she was angry all the time. Under those circumstances, I would be too.

"What about her will? Is she leaving them any money or anything else valuable?"

Liz shook her head again. "It's the daughters who pay her bills here. I don't think she has any money of her own, other than her Social Security check every month."

So much for that idea. "Does she have any particular enemy here at the home? Somebody she's really offended, rather than just pestered."

Liz took a minute to think about it. "I'm not sure," she said slowly. "Mrs. Good said she took her box of candy last week."

"Not really a killing offense, is it?" Richard said.

Liz shrugged. "Probably not, but you'd be surprised at how seriously our folks take that kind of thing. Mrs. Good's family sends her a box of candy every year, and she hoards it for a couple of months before she'll finish that last piece. It may not sound like a big deal to you, but you have to remember that Mrs. Good can't just drive to the mall to get another box. She's got arthritis so bad that she can't hardly stand up. That candy means a lot to her, and she was *so* got away with when it disappeared. She insisted that we search Mrs. Hamilton's room."

"Did you?"

"Yes, we did, just to reassure her. We got Mrs. Hamilton's

permission first, of course, and wasn't she furious! I think she said yes just to make Mrs. Good look bad. We searched everywhere, but couldn't find hide nor hair of it. And after all that, Mrs. Good still wouldn't believe it. She claimed that Mrs. Hamilton must have hid it somewhere else."

Mrs. Good's unreasonable anger sounded promising, but I couldn't honestly suspect her. "I can't see how a arthritic woman could have stabbed Mrs. Hamilton," I pointed out.

"I guess not," Liz said, and then she shook her head. "I don't know of anything else. Of course, the residents don't tell us everything that's going on."

"Why is that?" Richard asked

"Maybe they think that coming to a nurse would be like tattling," I guessed.

"That's part of it," Liz said. "And then I think they just like it this way because it gives them something to do. They'd rather fuss and fume among themselves." I must have frowned, because she added, "I'm not putting them down, really I'm not. Boredom is the biggest problem these people have. After a while, one day is an awful lot like another. If their feuds keep them entertained, who am I to interfere? Anyway, what I was leading up to is that maybe you should talk to one of the other residents."

"Is there anyone who was a particular friend of Mrs. Hamilton's?"

"Mr. Morgan would like to be, for some reason. The other nurses say he's been sweet on her ever since she got here, and no one can figure it out. She certainly doesn't encourage him. She's just as mean to him as she is to] everybody else."

"Could you find him and bring him here?" I asked.

"Sure."

She was gone long enough for me to ask Richard, "How am I doing?" and for him to reply, "'Exceeding wise, fair–spoken, and persuading.' *King Henry VIII*, Act IV, scene 2."

Then Liz brought in Mr. Morgan, performed introductions, and left. Mr. Morgan was thin but seemed heartier than most of the men in the home, and was dressed in a bright red pullover and gray slacks.

"Is Sadie all right?" he asked. "Liz wouldn't tell me a thing."

I weighed the idea of not telling him what was going on against the reality of my having no reason to ask him questions if something hadn't happened. Reality won. "Someone tried to kill Mrs. Hamilton," I said, watching his face for a reaction. All I saw was concern.

"Is she all right?"

"The doctor says she's going to be fine, but it was close."

He took a deep breath, and said, "Poor Sadie. First the stroke, and now this. Do they know who stabbed her?"

"I didn't say anything about stabbing," I said quickly. Was solving the crime going to be this easy? Of course not.

Mr. Morgan smiled. "Honey, this is a awful small place. Mrs. Robertson thought she saw blood when Sadie passed out, and Morris Nichols was watching when Liz pulled that knife out of the gift bag. We put two and two together a while ago, especially when no one would tell us anything different. We're not children."

"You're right," I said, acknowledging the reproof. "I'm sorry, but we didn't want to scare anybody until we had a better idea of what was going on. As soon as we're done here, I'll make some kind of an announcement."

"I think that would be a good idea. Now what did you want to talk to me about?"

"Did Liz tell you that Junior Norton deputized me?"

He nodded.

"What I'm trying to do is to take care of some of the groundwork for her, maybe find out who might have wanted to hurt Mrs. Hamilton. Liz tells me that you're pretty close to her."

Mr. Morgan leaned back in his chair. "Well, I don't know if you'd call us close. Sadie doesn't let anybody get too close."

"I understand that she can be difficult sometimes."

He grinned widely. "Difficult, my right eye. Sadie Hamilton is the most ornery woman I have ever met. Never has a nice word for anyone, and no one but her ever does anything right. She curses like a sailor, and I've never known her to pass up an chance to tell anybody just what she thinks about them."

"I expect she's nicer once you get to know her," I ventured.

"Not so you'd know it. She tells me off two, three times a day."

"Then why...?" I wasn't sure how to phrase the question.

"Then why did I put up with her? I like her, plain and simple. She keeps my blood moving. Sadie says I'm too damned nice, and I think she's right. My mama and daddy raised me to be polite, no matter what, and that's how I've always been. Not Sadie! She always says what's on her mind, lets it all hang out, like the young folks say now."

Actually, I hadn't known young folks to say that in quite some time, but I nodded anyway. "She sounds kind of like my Aunt Maggie. She's never been one to mince words either."

Mr. Morgan said, "Most of us old folks are too shy to speak our minds. We know we're in the way, so we act just as nice as we can to make sure people still want to be around us once in a while. Sadie just doesn't give a darn about what other people think." He looked at Richard. "You must know *The Taming of the Shrew*."

"'Her only fault, and that is faults enough, is that she is intolerable curst and shrewd and froward,'" Richard quoted. "Act I, scene 2."

"That's Sadie to a T. I never did like the end of that play, when Kate is all tamed. I'd just as soon she stayed a shrew, like Sadie has."

"Until she had the stroke, that is," I said.

He nodded sadly. "Oh, she's still got the feelings inside her, you saw that at the party. She just can't get the words out. It frustrates her something terrible. I pure hate to see her like that."

I realized that we had gotten off the track, and thought I better bring it back around to the attack on Mrs. Hamilton. "With her being so ill–tempered, do you think that there's someone she had particularly angered?"

He considered it for a minute, and then slowly shook his head. "I don't know a soul that really wants her dead, if that's what you mean. Sure she makes people mad, but not like that."

"Liz said something about Mrs. Good and a box of candy," I said, feeling silly.

Mr. Morgan waved away the suggestion. "Young lady, surely you don't think anybody stabbed Sadie over a box of candy."

"No, not really."

"And another thing," he continued, "Margaret Good had no business claiming it was Sadie who took that candy. She made such a big to–do over it when it came in the mail, showing everybody what a big box it was and talking about how generous her daughter was to send it. All along knowing that Sadie's brats don't so much as call her on the telephone, not even when they heard about the stroke. Margaret even left the box in the TV room to rub it in. If you ask me, it served her right when somebody made off with it."

"Was Mrs. Hamilton feuding with anybody else?" I asked.

"Before her stroke, she was on the outs with pretty much everybody," he said, grinning again. "Sadie told everyone in sight that Mrs. Houghton's husband used to run around on her, and Mrs. Houghton was right put out about that. Especially since it was true. Then Sadie threw out a vase of Charlie's flowers because she said she was allergic to them. And she got to the TV room first one morning a while back and insisted on watching game shows all day long when she knew a bunch of the other ladies wanted to watch their stories."

"Soap operas," I translated for Richard. He was rushing to write all of this down, but I didn't really think he needed to bother. I could see why Mrs. Hamilton hadn't been very popular, but none of this was exactly motive for murder.

"Anything else?" I asked.

"I think those are the most recent problems. If you want me to go back a few months or so—"

"No, I think this will be enough to start on. I appreciate your time, Mr. Morgan."

"That's all right, young lady. Do you think it would be all right if I went to see Sadie now?"

"I think she's still unconscious, but I guess it would be all right." Even if he was the one who tried to kill Mrs. Hamilton, he wasn't likely to overpower the nurse and Carlelle in order to try again.

Idelle and Odelle came in as Mr. Morgan left.

"Are you ready for us?" Odelle asked.

I nodded. "What did you find out?"

"It's hard to tell," Idelle said, "but I don't think anyone's been out of the parking lot since we came in. Other than Dr. Buchanan, that is. I suppose someone could have come in or out on foot, but it's awful slippery out there. I fell down twice myself."

"Are you all right?" I asked.

She rubbed her tail end. "Only hurt my dignity."

"What about the knife?" I said to Odelle.

"I talked to Mrs. Cummings the cook and she said they have a set of cooking knives just like the one you have. And there's one missing. It's been gone since last week, so she already bought herself a new one that has a different kind of handle."

Last week? That implied premeditation to me. "Did she have any idea of who could have taken it?"

Odelle shook her head. "She said they don't really lock up the kitchen, because there's never been any reason to. Residents come in for snacks all the time."

"So unless someone came in last week to steal the knife, and then managed to sneak back in tonight in the middle of an ice storm, it must have been one of the residents or a staff member," I said. That left out Clifford and the rest of my family out, I added to myself, but I had never really considered them suspects anyway.

Unfortunately, I was still stuck with every one of the residents and staff members who had been at the party. Plenty of suspects, but no motive.

"What do you want us to do now?" Odelle asked.

"Has Vasti got things under control back at the party?"

"You know she has," Idelle said with a snicker.

"Then maybe you two can go check with Carlelle in case she needs something to drink or to go to the bathroom."

They nodded and left.

"Well?" I said to Richard. "Any ideas?"

"We could bring in those soap opera fans. I know some people are ardently devoted to them."

"Thanks a whole lot. Next time you can be the deputy."

He shook his head emphatically. "No thank you. I'm quite content to play the role of faithful dogsbody."

I put my head on my hands. "What have we got here anyway? In a room full of people, someone stabs a little old lady through a wheelchair. Why stab her? I mean, she's a patient. Wouldn't it have been easier to slip something into her medication?"

"Not necessarily," Richard said. "Drugs are monitored pretty closely."

"OK. Then why in the party? Why not late at night?"

"The purloined letter approach? Whoever it was must have known that he or she wouldn't be noticed."

"Then why now? She just had a stroke, for heaven's sake. What harm could she do to anyone? I don't think she could even monopolize a television set the way she is now."

"Maybe she was an easier target. From what people have been telling us, how easy would it have been to sneak up on her before?"

I sighed. "Maybe Junior should have deputized Vasti instead of me because I haven't got a clue as to what's going on."

Richard put his arm around me. "You're doing fine. All Junior wanted you to do was to protect Mrs. Hamilton, and you're doing that. The rest is up to Junior, remember?"

"I guess," I said unwillingly. "It's just that it would be awfully nice to be able to hand the solution over to Junior when she gets here." I stood up. "Anyway, I promised Mr. Morgan I'd make that announcement. Coming, faithful dogsbody?"

"'I will follow you to the last gasp with truth and loyalty.' *As You Like It*, Act II, scene 3."

Word must have spread that I was playing detective because the people in the recreation room quieted down when Richard and I walked in. Vasti was doing her best to hand out more cookies, but I don't think anybody was taking her up on it. Clifford was playing a song over by the podium, and I waited until he finished before starting.

"Can I have everybody's attention?" I said unnecessarily, since they were all watching me already. "I'd like to make an announcement." The people moved closer. "Y'all probably all know about Mrs. Hamilton by now. She was stabbed, but she survived the attack. The doctor said she's going to be fine." I waited for that to sink in before going on. "Chief

Norton can't get through the storm to take charge herself, so she deputized me."

There was talking among them at that, and I thought I heard my grandfather's name mentioned. As I'd said earlier, there were no secrets in Byerly, so these people almost certainly knew I had taken an interest in such things before. Maybe that meant they'd trust me.

I continued, "I've been trying to see what I can find out about what happened, and that's where you folks come in. Did any of y'all see anyone around Mrs. Hamilton acting funny, someone who might have stabbed her?" There was a lot more talking, but no one seemed to have anything definite to say. "All right, then how about this? The knife used to stab Mrs. Hamilton was stuck in this bag afterwards." I held up the gift bag. "Did any of you see someone messing with this bag or putting anything into it?" Again the response was negative. I was disappointed but not surprised. If anyone had seen anything, word would already have reached me.

I went on, "Now you folks know as much as I do, but I'll answer any questions you might have."

A fearful-looking woman raised her hand, and I nodded at her. "How do we know that the murderer isn't going to come after someone else?"

I did feel right foolish when she asked that. Until then I had just assumed Mrs. Hamilton was the only target, and I didn't have any real reason for thinking that. Foolish or not, I didn't suppose it would be very comforting for me to admit my mistake. "That's why we've been keeping all of you in here," I improvised. "Safety in numbers."

A man muttered, "Safety in numbers didn't help Sadie Hamilton."

"That's because she wasn't expecting anything. Now all of you are on your guard."

"Does that mean that the murderer is still here?" the first woman asked. "Here in this room?"

There was no way around that one. "I'm afraid that's just what I mean. As far as we can tell, no one has left the home since Mrs. Hamilton was stabbed."

Now there was a wave of muttering and sidelong glances. I wanted to reassure them, but I resisted. These people deserved the truth. I didn't expect whoever it was to go after another target, but I couldn't be sure.

I looked at a clock on the wall. It was close to midnight, and these folks were going to have to go to bed soon. How could I protect so many of them?

"It's getting late," I said, "and I know you're getting tired." Goodness knows I was. "My cousins, my husband, and I are going to stay here for the night." I probably should have checked with them first, but between the ice on the roads and a thwarted murderer in the building, I didn't imagine that they'd argue. "I think we should all spend the night in here." There was some comments made, both from nurses and residents, but I talked over them. Hospital beds had wheels, didn't they? "We'll just roll in beds, and stick together. Nobody else is going to get hurt."

There was a lot of conversation, but I didn't hear any loud objections so I decided I was going to get away with it.

"Liz, Vasti, and Clifford are going to be in charge of getting everybody everything they have to have for tonight, so if there's something special you need, just tell them."

Clifford looked blank, but Vasti called out, "People, I'd appreciate it if you'd go sit down until we get things set up." There was some movement, but clearly not enough to suit Vasti. "Come on now!" she said, clapping her hands sharply. "We haven't got all night."

This sounded like as good a time as any for me to leave, and I pulled Richard along with me.

He asked, "Where to now, fearless leader?"

"I'm not that fearless," I answered. "I want to get out of here before Vasti comes up with something for me to do."

The door to the infirmary was flanked by two of the triplets. I know they were trying hard to look menacing, but it just didn't work with those elf costumes.

"How's she doing?" I asked.

"She was stirring a bit a little while ago," Carlelle said.

"I think she might be awake by now," said Odelle. "Are you going to interrogate her?"

I nodded, and opened the door as quietly as I could. The had opened the curtain around Mrs. Hamilton's bed to give them more room. A nurse I didn't know and Idelle looked up as I came in, and I saw that Mr. Morgan was sitting by the bed holding Mrs. Hamilton's hand.

Richard tapped my shoulder and mouthed that he was going to stay outside, and I closed the door behind me. "How is she doing?" I whispered.

"I think she's waking up," Mr. Morgan said. "Are you going to question her?"

"I'm going to try," I said. "Do you think you could stay and interpret for me? She was pretty hard to understand earlier."

"Certainly."

Idelle and the nurse moved out of the way, and I pulled a chair up to the bed. Mrs. Hamilton did seem to be moving restlessly, and I hadn't been there but a few minutes when she opened her eyes.

She glared accusingly at me, then gave Mr. Morgan a somewhat friendlier look and mumbled something.

"She wants to know what she's doing here," Mr. Morgan said. "What should I tell her?"

"You know her better than I do. Do you think she can handle the truth?"

He nodded. "A lot better than she could our *not* telling her." Then to Mrs. Hamilton he said, "Sadie, this is kind of hard to believe."

She mumbled something else, and even without understanding the words I could tell she was impatient.

Mr. Morgan said, "Sadie, somebody stabbed you. Somebody tried to kill you."

She didn't say anything for a while, and I was trying to decide if she had understood him or not when she blurted out, "Who?"

"We don't know who," I said. "We were hoping you could tell us. Somebody came up behind you at the party. Did you see anybody?"

She shook her head, and said, "Die?"

I smiled in what I thought was a reassuring manner. "No, ma'am, the doctor says you're going to be just fine." Her glare told me that she was not reassured, but I thought I knew why. "Don't worry. We're going to make sure that no one hurts you again." I was wrong.

In the clearest words I had heard from her, she said, "Should have let him kill me."

I looked at Mr. Morgan in shock, and he started wringing Mrs. Hamilton's hand. "Sadie, don't say things like that!"

Her only response was to pull her hand away from his and determinedly shut her eyes.

The nurse and Idelle were both shaking their heads sadly, and Mr. Morgan kept whispering, "Sadie? Sadie?" I didn't have anything else to say, so I just left.

"You be sure and stay with her," I said to Carlelle and Odelle. They grinned and saluted, but I knew they'd stay.

"Well?" Richard asked once we were out of earshot. "Any accusations?"

"She said she didn't see anything, but I don't think she would have told me if she had. Richard, she *wants* to die!" I was on the verge of tears, and I guess Richard realized it.

"Come on," he said. "Let's find someplace quiet." He led me into what looked like a nurse's lounge, sat me down on a couch, and put his arms around me.

I took half a dozen deep breaths to fight back the tears. "It was so awful," I said. "She actually said that we should have let whoever it was finish the job. We're doing all we can to protect her, and she doesn't even want to be protected. How can she give up like that?"

"She's old," Richard reminded me. "According to Mr. Morgan, she's been miserable ever since her stroke. It's not unusual for people to get depressed at a time like that."

"I know, but it's Christmas."

"More people get depressed during the holidays than at any other time of the year."

"I know," I said again. "But..." Then I stopped. Was what Mrs. Hamilton was feeling all that different from what I had been feeling? And she had a whole lot more reason to be depressed than I did. My grandfather was dead, it was true, but he would have been the last person on earth to want me moping around. Suddenly I felt very ashamed, both for blaming Sadie Hamilton for her depression and for wallowing in my own. "I really have been a Scrooge this year, haven't I?"

"Where did that come from?"

"Just thinking about Mrs. Hamilton. It's hard to explain, and right now we've got work to do."

"Are you sure you're all right?"

"*I'm* not giving up. Maybe if Mrs. Hamilton sees how hard we're working, she'll realize she's got something to live for."

"Maybe," Richard said, "but don't count on it. This is Byerly, not 34th Street."

I nodded, but I don't suppose I really believed him. I wanted a Christmas miracle for Mrs. Hamilton and maybe a little one for myself while I was at it.

Vasti spotted us as soon as we came back into the recreation room and gestured for us to join her.

"You go ahead," Richard said. "Surely someone must need me to lift a bed or something."

"Coward!" I said to his back.

"'The better part of valour is discretion.' *King Henry IV, Part I*, Act V, scene 4."

Vasti really had got the job done. The party food and tables were gone, and the room was filled with rows of beds. A line of curtained panels ran down the center and two signs pointedly labeled the halves LADIES and GENTLE-MEN. A few folks were already pulling off their shoes and socks and climbing into bed.

After all her hard work, I couldn't very well ignore her demand for my attention. "Vasti, you have done a wonderful job."

"Oh this," she said waving her hand airily. "Nothing to it. What I wanted to tell you is that I think I solved the case!"

"Really?" I said, hoping I didn't sound too sarcastic.

If I had, she didn't notice it. "Look what I found!" She held out a Whitman's Sampler box of candy.

I guess I looked blank.

"This box of candy was stolen from Mrs. Good. A nurse saw it and told me all about it. You see—"

"I've heard the story. Are you sure that's the same box?" I said, not sure why I should care.

"Mrs. Good identified it herself, and I had the devil of a time convincing her that she couldn't have it back."

"Why couldn't she?"

"It's evidence," she said as if it were the most obvious thing in the world. "I found it in Mrs. Hamilton's room."

Now that was interesting, although puzzling. Hadn't Liz told me that they had searched the room when the candy went missing?

"Her room is one of the closest, so I thought we could wheel her bed in here. She's not going to be using it tonight, after all. Anyway, this was in the drawer of her nightstand."

I didn't even bother asking Vasti what she had been doing in the nightstand. "So you think the candy has something to do with the attack?" I said.

"It must have. And there's more." She lifted the lid of the box, and I saw that there was only one piece of candy missing. "Look at that piece there," Vasti said, pointing to a nougat.

I did so, careful not to touch. "What?"

"Just look."

I got closer, and saw what I thought was a fingerprint. "It looks like someone picked it up." Knowing Vasti, I was pretty sure I knew who it had been.

"It's been tampered with," Vasti said triumphantly. "It looked funny to me, and when I looked on the bottom, I found a needle mark. Don't you see? It's been poisoned."

"Did you get one of the nurses to take a look?"

"Of course not. One of them might be the murderer."

She had a point, of course.

"Pick it up and see for yourself," Vasti said.

"No, I trust you, and I don't want to disturb any evidence. If it was tampered with, what do you suppose it means?"

"Isn't it obvious? It means that Mrs. Hamilton was intending to poison Mrs. Good, and Mrs. Good retaliated."

"Vasti," I said slowly, "do you really think Mrs. Good could have stabbed someone?"

"Well, maybe not. But it has to be connected somehow."

"Maybe," I conceded. "If it has been poisoned, I'd think that a more likely idea would be that someone had tried to kill Mrs. Hamilton before and hadn't succeeded."

"That could be it, I suppose," Vasti said grudgingly.

"I'll tell you what. You hang on to the candy, and we'll have Junior send it to a lab for testing. They'll be able to tell us for sure."

"All right," Vasti said, somewhat mollified, and went to tell an orderly what he was doing wrong.

By then the residents were pretty much settled down for the night. The nurses and orderlies were stationed in chairs throughout the room, making sure everyone was taken care of. I saw that Clifford had pulled up a chair right next to

Liz's, and while they weren't speaking, the way they were looking at each other said a lot.

"How's it going?" I asked them.

"Pretty well, I guess," Liz said. "Maybe they'll get some sleep, anyway. Clifford was a big help." She smiled at him, and he smiled back. "They'd be a lot happier if Chief Norton was here. No offense, Laurie Anne."

"No offense taken. I'd rather that Junior was here, too."

I saw Vasti supervising Richard, who was shoving in a chair I recognized as coming from Dr. Buchanan's office. "I don't know about you people," she said, "but I'm worn out." She plopped down onto the chair, and leaned back. "I'm going to try to get some sleep."

I thought longingly of one of the other chairs from that office, but said, "The triplets worked all day, and I know they're beat, too. I better take over so they can get some rest."

"I don't think so," Richard said. "I think you should get yourself a chair and grab forty or fifty winks. I'll stay with Mrs. Hamilton."

"Are you sure?"

"Absolutely." He pulled a worn paperback of *The Winter's Tale* out of his back pocket. "The Bard and I will keep watch together."

I gave him a hug and a kiss. "You are wonderful, you know."

"'The naked truth,'" he said with a grin. "*Love's Labour's Lost*, Act V, scene 2." He bowed with a flourish before he left.

By the time the triplets arrived, I had found chairs for all of us and they quickly wrapped themselves in blankets Liz produced and fell asleep. I must admit thinking that it was ridiculous that anyone could sleep in a situation like this, but I only had time to think about it for a minute before dozing off myself.

I awoke to a loud whisper. "Nurse! Come here!"

Liz muttered, "Now what?" and tiptoed her way toward a bed next to the window. A minute later she was back. "Mr. Biggers said he saw someone walk by the window."

"Is he sure?" I asked.

"Positive. I had to promise him that we'd go check or he'd be on his way out there himself."

I looked toward the window unenthusiastically, not thrilled by the idea of going out in the cold and ice, when darned if I didn't see a shadow myself. "I think there is someone there!"

Liz shrank back toward Clifford. "Maybe it's the murderer. What are we going to do?"

"I guess I'm going to go see who it is," Clifford said in a much deeper voice than he generally used. "Have y'all got any kind of a gun around here?"

Liz shook her head. "There's a softball bat in with the sports equipment."

"That'll do. You two better stay here and keep an eye out."

"Clifford," Liz said, her hand on his arm. "You aren't going out there alone, are you?"

"No, he's not," I said firmly. I was older than he was, and if anything happened to him, his mother would kill me. "I'm going, too. Liz, I wouldn't wake the others until we know for sure what's going on."

"That's right," Clifford said. "We don't want to make too much noise. That might warn him."

Common sense told me that making noise was exactly what we should do, so our prowler would pick up and go, but I was still hoping to solve the puzzle for Junior. Besides, I rationalized, who was I to spoil Clifford's big moment?

Liz watched him adoringly as we armed ourselves with aluminum softball bats and put on our coats. "Be careful," she whispered after us. Well, after Clifford anyway.

"You stay behind me," Clifford said as we stepped out onto the icy sidewalk, and I saw no reason to argue with him. Just staying upright was taking all of my attention, and I cursed myself for not finding something to put on my feet instead of those darned elf shoes.

We walked around the building as quietly as we could. I wasn't sure, but from the broken ice, it did look like someone had walked down the sidewalk ahead of us. We were just about even with Mr. Biggers's window when I saw a large figure walking slowly, peering into windows.

I tugged at Clifford's sleeve but he'd seen him, too. He gestured me forward, and together we crept closer. Only I guess we weren't creeping quietly enough, because suddenly the prowler turned right toward us.

Clifford raised his bat threateningly, and called out, "You over there! What are you doing here?"

The man said, "Hey now, put that down," and stepped into the light.

I started laughing. Our prowler was wearing a red hat with white trim and had a long, white beard. That's right— it was Santa Claus.

It wasn't really Santa Claus, of course. After a minute more I recognized Vasti's husband. "Arthur? What on earth are you doing out here?"

"I know I'm late," he said, coming toward us. "I got stuck in the ice. I'd have gone on home, but I saw Vasti's car in the parking lot and thought the party must still be going on. I was hoping I could get her attention from out here."

"Why didn't you just come on inside?" Clifford wanted to know.

"Vasti told me not to let anyone see me before we made our big entrance. I wasn't sure if she'd still want me to give out presents or not."

We started back for the front door. "I'm afraid you're way too late to give out presents," I said, and then stopped.

"What's the matter?" Clifford asked.

"Presents," I said softly. "Where was her present?"

Arthur said, "Whose present?"

"Mrs. Hamilton's!" I said. "Come on!"

We went as fast as we could, and I threw off my coat and dropped it on the floor in my hurry to get back to where Vasti was sleeping.

Liz looked up as soon as I came in, but I went right past her. Let Clifford explain, I thought, as I went to shake my cousin. "Vasti! Wake up!"

"What? What's going on?"

"I need your Secret Santa list."

"What for?" I saw her clipboard under her chair and grabbed it. "Is this it?" Without waiting for an answer, I started flipping through the pages. I found the list of residents, the gifts they wanted, and their Secret Santas. "Thank goodness you're organized," I said to Vasti, and looked for Mrs. Hamilton's entry. There it was, in black and white. I can't say that it was the name I expected, but it did make sense once I found it. Especially when I thought about the candy.

By now Arthur and Clifford had caught up with me, and were greeting and being greeted by their significant others.

"Clifford," Liz said, "are you all right? I was so worried." She looked up at him, and he took her in his arms. No mistletoe was required for the kiss that followed.

"Arthur? Where in the Sam Hill have you been?" Vasti said. "And straighten that beard. You look silly."

I left them to their explanations, and went to the infirmary. I took my time, because I wanted to think about just what I was going to say when I got there. I tapped lightly on the door, and Richard let me in.

"What's up?" he asked.

"I think I've got it," I said quietly.

The nurse had that dazed look of someone staying awake by main force of will. "You can go grab a cup of coffee if you want," I said. She didn't ask for explanations, just nodded and went out.

Mr. Morgan was still perched by Mrs. Hamilton's bed, watching her sleep. "How is she?" I asked.

"'O sleep, O gentle sleep, nature's soft nurse!'" Richard said. "*King Henry VI*, Part II, Act III, scene 1."

"We better wake her up," I said.

"Wake her up?" Mr. Morgan said. "What for?"

"She needs to know who it was that tried to kill her," I said.

"I'm awake," a churlish voice said from the bed.

Sure enough, Mrs. Hamilton was glaring at us all. "Good," I said, and took the nurse's chair.

"Mrs. Hamilton," I said, "I think I know who tried to kill you, but I need to ask you something first." Her only response was a grunt, but she didn't take her eyes off of me.

"My cousin found Mrs. Good's box of candy in your room. Did you take it?"

I could tell from the way her face turned red what she was going to say before said it. "*No!*"

"That's what I thought. I'm guessing that someone left that box in your room a week or so ago. Is that right?"

She looked suspicious, but she nodded.

"There was one piece missing from the box. Did you eat it?"

She made a face. "Half. Tasted bad."

"I imagine it did. It had been tampered with."

"Poison?" she wanted to know.

"I think so."

She blinked several times. "Who?"

I didn't answer her directly. Instead I looked up at Frank Morgan, who had been listening attentively. "Maybe Mr. Morgan will tell us."

He got very still. "How would I know?"

"Or maybe you'd rather tell us what you got Mrs. Hamilton for Christmas."

He didn't say anything, so I went on.

"I checked Vasti's list, and you were Mrs. Hamilton's Secret Santa. Only there wasn't any gift for her under the tree. And you weren't on the triplets' shopping list, because you told Vasti you'd get her something yourself. What did you get her?"

"Nothing," he said. "She didn't want anything."

"Didn't she? Is that what she said?"

He looked down at his hands for a long moment, then shook his head and looked at Mrs. Hamilton while he answered me. "You don't know what's it like, you *can't* know.

Sadie's an old woman, but she's always been strong and independent. She didn't like being here, but she could stand it as long as she could keep doing for herself. Then she had the stroke, and she couldn't even go to the bathroom by herself anymore. Most of her body is just dead." He looked up at me. "Do you know how you'd feel if you were in that shape?"

I shook my head.

"I'll tell you how you'd feel. You'd want to die, just like Sadie did. She wanted to die worse than anything. She wouldn't fill out a gift list, said she didn't care. I went to her and asked her if there wasn't something I could get for her. She looked me straight in the eye and said as clear as could be, 'I want to die.'"

He took a deep breath. "Don't think it was easy for me to do, because it wasn't. It was the hardest thing I've ever done in my life, but I couldn't just leave her like that. I took Mrs. Good's candy and put a sedative in it because I thought Sadie would go easy, that they'd think she went in her sleep. I didn't realize it would taste bad. I just thought it hadn't worked, and that's when I decided to steal that knife and use it. I thought that way she'd die quickly, but I guess I didn't hit the right spot."

He looked back at Mrs. Hamilton, who was watching us carefully with her one good eye. "I sharpened it up as good as I could, and made sure to hit you on the side with no feeling so it wouldn't hurt. I didn't want it to hurt." His voice broke. "I'm sorry, Sadie, I wanted to help you and I've only made it worse."

Mrs. Hamilton struggled for a moment, and finally said, "Jail?"

"That's right. I'll be going to jail."

"For me?"

"I'm not sure I follow you."

"Jail? For me?"

He looked at me, and I said, "I think she's asking if you were willing to go to jail for her."

Mrs. Hamilton nodded as hard as she could in confirmation.

Mr. Morgan said, "I guess you could say that. To be honest, I was hoping it wouldn't come to that." To me he added, "I would have confessed if it looked like anyone else was going to get into trouble."

I nodded, believing him.

"For me?" Mrs. Hamilton said, and she sounded almost in awe. Her next sentence was garbled, but I think she said, "No one does things for me."

"That's not true, Sadie," Mr. Morgan protested. "Lots of people do things for you."

She shook her head. "You. You tried. For me. Why?"

Mr. Morgan cocked his head. "Because I thought that's what you wanted. I care for you, Sadie, you must know that. And it's Christmas. I wanted to you to have what you wanted."

"Did want it," Mrs. Hamilton said. "Not now. Don't want it. Live."

Mr. Morgan took her hand in his. "Really, Sadie? I'm so glad."

I halfway expected her to jerk her hand away from him, but she didn't. Instead she fixed her eye on me and said, "Jail?"

"He'll be going to jail all right."

"No!" she said vehemently.

"You don't want him to go to jail?" I asked, wanting to be sure she meant what I thought she meant.

She shook her head vigorously. "No jail."

Mr. Morgan looked astonished. "Sadie, are you sure?"

"No jail." Then to me, she said, "You fix."

"Mrs. Hamilton, I don't know what I can do. I'm not really a deputy."

"No jail. Fix it!" Then she closed her eyes. Even in that condition, she had dismissed me as plain as day.

Mr. Morgan looked at me. "Can you do that?"

I thought about it a minute. "Well, since Mrs. Hamilton is still alive, I don't know that Junior can do anything without her pressing charges. I expect she'll want to have a good long talk with you, though." I hesitated. "Assuming that this is the first time you've ever tried anything like this, that is."

"Of course it is!" he said. "What kind of person do you think I am?" He glared at me for a minute, and then relented. "I suppose you had to ask that. I swear, I never tried to kill anyone before."

"All right," I said. Of course, I was going to warn Junior to check over the nursing home's records just to be sure that there hadn't been any suspicious deaths, but I didn't see any reason to mention that.

I called the nurse back in and decided that she would be enough protection for Mrs. Hamilton now. Richard and I deserved the rest. Which, unfortunately, we were not going to get for a while yet.

We had barely got back to the recreation room and found empty chairs when we saw blue lights flashing from the parking lot. Junior had finally arrived. She had thoughtfully not used the siren so the others kept on sleeping, but I knew that she was going to want me awake to catch her up.

It didn't really take all that long to tell, once Junior quit laughing over the elf suit I had nearly forgotten I was still wearing. "I think that's about it," I said. "If I remember anything else, I'll let you know."

Junior just kept shaking her head. "I knew you'd try, but I didn't have any idea that you'd put it together so quick."

Quick? It felt like I had been at the nursing home for days. "What are you going to do about Mr. Morgan?"

"Well, I'm going to have to talk to Mrs. Hamilton myself, but if she really doesn't want to press charges, I expect I'll be able to find some loophole or another."

"Good. And now I would like to formally resign my position of acting deputy."

"Resignation accepted, but don't expect any kind of severance pay."

"No? Did I not do a good job?"

"You did fine," she said, "but you're out of uniform." She started snickering again.

"Ha ha," I said, with very little good humor. Then, to change the subject, I asked, "Did you get that baby delivered all right?"

"The mama did all the hard work. About all I did was catch the daddy when he passed out. A healthy girl, by the way. They were all set to name it after me until they found out what my name is."

"Junior Junior wasn't quite what they had in mind?"

"Not hardly."

I yawned so wide it almost hurt. "How are the roads?"

"Getting better," she said. "You shouldn't have any trouble driving now if you take it slow, and the ice will probably all be gone by afternoon."

"Good," I said.

"I expect you want to get some sleep," she said. "I know I do."

"That's part of it," I said, and indeed the first part of my plan was to take off the elf suit and climb into bed. But after I got some rest, I was going Christmas shopping.

Marley's Ghost

This story takes place in the time gap between the second and third Laura Fleming novels: Dead Ringer *and* Trouble Looking for a Place to Happen.

The Walters family of Walters Mill might be Scrooges for most of the year, but when it came to the Christmas party, they really did it up right: fancy decorations, an open bar, plenty of tasty refreshments, and a disk jockey to play dance music. Even though I was there with my cousin Thaddeous instead of my husband Richard, I would have had myself a good old time if I hadn't been so concerned with trying to figure out who murdered Fannie Topper.

Instead of having fun, I was devoting my attention to the three men that could have killed her. I didn't really expect any of them to confess, of course. The idea was to try to figure out a motive for the killing.

First I chatted with Joe Bowley over plates of ham and roast beef. He looked like a man who enjoyed his food, but didn't mind talking while he ate. Of course I couldn't just casually bring up the subject of a murder that happened twenty-five years ago, so I got him to discuss barbeque. I thought that it would eventually lead to Fannie Topper's barbeque place, but no such luck. I don't know if he avoided talking about Fannie on purpose or not, but he went on and on about Buck Overton's in Mt. Airy, which he hadn't even been to since before Fannie was killed.

Next I tried dancing with Bobby Plummer, and I had to admit that he was a real good dancer. He was light on his feet and smiled gallantly when I stepped on his toes. He didn't hold me so tight the way some men try to do, which made me wonder if the rumors about him being gay were true. Maybe he was just being polite. Bobby was in much better shape than Joe, so with him, I asked about exercise. Specifically, playing baseball. I thought sure that he'd mention the championship the Walters Mill team had won all those years ago, the party afterwards, and the murder after that. Nope. He talked about NordicTrack.

Finally I sat on the edge of the hall with Pete Fredericks. Getting him to talk about death was no problem, but it wasn't what I had in mind. It seemed that Pete was going to be leaving the mill soon to work with one of Byerly's morticians. I learned lots about what happened to people after death, but nothing about how one particular woman came to die.

When the party ended, I didn't know a bit more than I had before I got there. And it was only two days before Christmas.

If I had had the sense God gave a milk cow, I told myself, I would have just bought Aunt Edna a sweater or a nightgown when I drew her name that Christmas. But no, I had to get it into my head that I was going to give her something she really wanted. That meant solving a twenty–five–year–old murder and laying Marley's ghost to rest.

I got the idea the day after Richard and I arrived in Byerly for Christmas, and I went to pay my duty call on Aunt Edna. If it had been Aunt Nora or Aunt Daphine, or almost any other Burnette, I'd have just tapped on the front door and walked in. But this was Aunt Edna's house, so I rang the doorbell and waited for her to answer.

She opened the door so quickly that I knew she must have heard me drive up. "Hey, Laurie Anne. Come on in. Where's Richard?"

"He snuck off to finish his Christmas shopping." I knew that the prospect of spending time with Aunt Edna had been the real reason my husband couldn't wait to shop, and given a choice, I'd have gone with him. It's not that I didn't like Aunt Edna, exactly, but she and I had never been close. Other than being related, we didn't seem to have a whole lot in common.

We hugged briefly in the hall, and then she took my coat to hang up.

"You're wearing an awful light jacket for this time of year," she said. "Aren't you cold?"

"I guess I've gotten used to the winters up North." After several years in Boston, December in North Carolina seemed almost warm in comparison.

"Why don't you go have a seat in the living room, and I'll get us some hot chocolate."

"That would be nice."

It felt funny to be waiting in the living room like I was company. Any of my other aunts would have invited me into the kitchen instead of leaving me alone like that.

The room was chilly because it wasn't used often, but there wasn't a speck of dust anywhere. I never have understood the idea of keeping a room pristine for company, but obviously Aunt Edna did. Every chair was angled just so, and each sofa pillow was stiffly placed.

The only friendly touch was the row of Christmas cards taped along the mantel, and rather than disturb those pillows, I went to look and see who had sent them. There was the funny snowman that Richard and I had sent, a sweet–faced Madonna from Aunt Ruby Lee, a cheerful Santa Claus from Aunt Nora, and a pretty snow scene from Aunt Daphine.

There was one particularly elaborate card with a pear tree decorated with turtledoves, pipers piping, and representatives of the other days of Christmas. I looked inside and read the message: "Merry Christmas. I hope things have gone well for you." It was signed Caleb.

Caleb? I didn't know any Caleb. Did Aunt Edna have a new beau? I didn't think it was very likely. There was a photo of Aunt Edna on top of the mantel, and I couldn't help but compare the young woman in the picture to the older woman who had met me at the door. Somehow she had changed from slender to skinny, and the fine hair that had flowed over her shoulders was now tightly pinned into a bun.

Aunt Edna brought in two mugs of hot chocolate. "Here you go," she said.

"Thank you."

We sat down on the couch and sipped.

"How have you been doing, Aunt Edna?"

"Fair to middling. Yourself?"

"About the same. Have you got your Christmas shopping done?"

"Pretty much. How about you?"

"I have a few pieces to pick up yet." As a matter of fact, I still had to find a gift for Aunt Edna. Since there were so many Burnettes, we didn't try to buy gifts for everybody. Instead we drew names, and ever since Thanksgiving I had been trying to come up with something my aunt would want. "Whenever I go into the stores, I keep finding things I want for myself instead of for the one I'm shopping for," I said subtly. "Don't you hate it when that happens?"

"I haven't seen much that interested me this year," she said.

So much for subtlety. I took a big swallow of hot chocolate, and wondered how long I'd have to stay before I could exit gracefully.

"Did you put your Christmas tree in the den?" I asked, since there wasn't one visible.

"I didn't bother with one this year. Just me by myself, it doesn't seem worth the trouble. Nora will have one for Christmas morning."

"A tree is a lot of work," I agreed, thinking of the live tree Richard and I had put up right after Thanksgiving so we'd have time to enjoy it before coming down for Christmas. "Your cards are pretty."

That got a little smile out of her. "I do enjoy getting Christmas cards," she said. "Of course, people don't send them like they used to. They cost so much now."

"That's true." I snuck a look at my watch. Only ten minutes gone.

"How's work?" Aunt Edna asked, and I gratefully launched into a description of my latest project. I know she wasn't really interested in the advantages and disadvantages of programming in Visual Basic, but I figured that anything was better than dead silence. I finally stopped when I saw her eyes start to glaze over.

"And Richard?" she prompted. "How is his work?"

That gave me a chance for another monologue. Then I asked about her son Linwood, his wife Sue, and their kids. That helped a little. Then she caught me up on her church activities, the real focus of her life.

Another look at my watch. We were now up to twenty–five minutes, and had already exhausted our best topics. I'd have even welcomed her asking me when Richard and I were going to start a family, a question I usually dread. Instead, we fell into a strained silence. There are companionable silences where people just enjoy each other's company, but this wasn't one of them.

In desperation, I looked up at her Christmas cards again. "Who's Caleb?"

Aunt Edna started so hard that she spilled hot chocolate on her dress. "What?"

"That card is signed 'Caleb,'" I said, surprised that the question had caused such a reaction. "I was just wondering who he is."

She stared at the card. "Just a friend. An old friend. Somebody I used to know."

That was the last time during that interminable hour that Aunt Edna seemed to know I was there. Oh, she said the right things at the right times and she offered me more hot chocolate, but I could tell that her mind wasn't in the same room as I was. It was a relief when enough time passed that I could politely leave.

❧

After that, I couldn't wait to get to Aunt Nora's, where I walked right in, got enthusiastic hugs from Aunt Nora, Uncle Buddy, and cousins Thaddeous and Willis, and was promptly installed in the kitchen with more hot chocolate. Aunt Nora was shorter and rounder than Aunt Edna, kept her hair nicely styled and dyed, and she smiled all the time. Even her hot chocolate was sweeter.

After we had gone through the preliminaries of work and gossip, I asked, "Aunt Nora, do you have any idea of what I can get Aunt Edna for Christmas? I can't think of a thing."

"Well, you could get her a sweater. Or a nightgown is always good."

"Didn't Ilene get her a nightgown last year? And I know Carlelle got her a sweater the year before that."

"And I gave her a nightgown and robe myself three years ago," Aunt Nora said. "Edna's not easy to shop for."

"I'll say." Then I remembered that odd Christmas card. "Do you know somebody named Caleb? A friend of Aunt Edna's?"

She didn't jump like Aunt Edna had, but she did look mighty surprised. "Caleb? She used to know a Caleb. Why do you ask?"

"She got a Christmas card from him. When I asked her

who it was, she acted real strange, and I just wondered why."

"Surely it can't be *that* Caleb," she said, more to herself than to me. "What did the card say?"

"'Merry Christmas and I hope things have worked out all right.' Something like that. Who in the Sam Hill is Caleb?"

"Caleb is Edna's ex–boyfriend. One of them, anyway. She dated lots of fellows, but Caleb was the one she fell for. She's never been the same since they broke up."

"Aunt Edna dated around?"

"Oh yes. She was the most popular one of us sisters. Your mama was the smart one, just like you. Nellie was the dreamer, Ruby Lee was the pretty one, Daphine was the one with common sense, and I was the hard worker. But Edna—she was the one with spirit. You should have seen her. She was a pistol."

"*My* Aunt Edna?"

"You young people think the world didn't exist until you came along," she said, shaking her head. "You never knew the Edna I grew up with. All the boys were crazy about her, and she broke half a dozen hearts before she decided just which one she wanted. And that was Caleb."

"So what happened?"

"Caleb left Byerly a long time ago. After Fannie Topper died."

"Fannie Topper?" That name sounded familiar. So did Caleb's, now that I heard it in that context. "You're not talking about Caleb *Wilkins*, are you? The one who killed Fannie Topper?"

Every kid in Byerly knew about Marley's ghost. Fannie Topper used to run a barbeque and beer joint in Marley, the black section of Byerly. One night her little boy Tim came downstairs looking for her and found a man standing by her dead body, covered in blood. They say Fannie didn't believe in banks and she had a lot of money hidden somewhere, and that the man came looking for it. When she caught him, he killed her. Since nobody but Fannie knew where the money was hidden, it was never recovered. The story was that her ghostly figure appeared either to guard the money or to show somebody where it was, depending on who was telling it.

The man found over Fannie's body was Caleb Wilkins.

"He was found not guilty," Aunt Nora said firmly.

"I know, but everybody always said that the only reason he got off was because there wasn't enough evidence."

"Well, everybody saying something doesn't make it so. I didn't think he did it then, and I don't think so now. More importantly, Edna never thought Caleb did it."

"The trial and all must have been awful for her."

"Well, it wasn't easy to get through, I can tell you that. Of course, all of us Burnettes knew he didn't do it, and when he was found not guilty, we thought it was all over and that he and Edna were going to live happily ever after."

"What happened?"

"What happened is that the people in this town drove Caleb away. They started walking by him on the street like he wasn't there, and whispering behind his back, and things like that. Oh, not everybody, but enough that he said he didn't feel at home here anymore. Can you imagine that? His family had been in Byerly for years and years."

"So he left town."

She nodded. "It was just about this time of year when

the trial ended and Caleb saw how people were going to be treating him for the rest of his life. He came over to the house Christmas day and we sang carols and ate Mama's coconut cake and visited. That evening, we sisters played music on the record player so we could dance."

She looked up at me. "You were there, too. Just a little thing, and your mama and daddy were holding you between them so the three of you could dance together. Then Paw took you so they could dance." She smiled, remembering that night. I wished that I could remember it, too. My parents and grandfather were gone now, and I still missed them, especially at Christmas.

"Anyway, it got late and Edna went out on the porch with Caleb to kiss him good night. Then he left. The next morning Paw gave her a letter, said that Caleb had asked him to give it to her."

"What did it say?"

"It was Caleb saying goodbye to Edna. He said he couldn't stay in Byerly anymore, that he had to make a fresh start. He said he couldn't ask her to come with him, not when he didn't know where he was going or how he was going to make a living, so he thought it was best to just go alone. He said he hoped her life would be everything she had ever dreamed about."

Aunt Nora was quiet for a long time, and I finally asked, "Didn't she try to find him?"

"Lord no! She didn't *want* to find him. After she read that letter, she was so mad that she ripped it into little bitty pieces. Then she threw it and everything he had ever given her into the trash can. Every bit of it."

"I can't imagine Aunt Edna that angry."

"Laurie Anne, I'd never seen anybody so fired up. Here she had stayed with him all through his being arrested and in jail and on trial. When people stared at them on the street, she stared right back. She did all that for him, and then he up and left her. If he had come back that same day, I think she would have slammed the door right in his face."

"Do you think she would have gone with him if he had asked?"

"I know she would have. She loved him that much. But he didn't ask. It wasn't long afterwards that she started dating Loman, and they were engaged within the month and married that summer. You know how things turned out with them."

I knew that Loman hadn't been much of a husband to Aunt Edna, and I was fairly sure that she was better off now that he was dead.

As if guessing my thoughts, Aunt Nora shrugged and said, "Maybe Loman wasn't the best man in the world, but at least he was here. Still, I don't think Edna ever got over Caleb."

After that we talked about other things, but now I was preoccupied, just like Aunt Edna had been. Only I wasn't dreaming about a lost love; I was thinking that I had stumbled on something I could give Aunt Edna for Christmas.

"I never would have guessed that Aunt Edna had a past," Richard said after I got back to Aunt Maggie's house and told him the story.

Actually, first I gave my lanky, dark–haired husband a

hug and a kiss. Then I asked him where Aunt Maggie was, and found out that after she made sure that he still knew where the kitchen and the bathroom were, she had headed out. Aunt Maggie sold collectibles at flea markets and auctions, and Christmas was such a busy time for her that we probably wouldn't even see her until Christmas day. That's one reason Richard and I liked staying with her when we came to Byerly. She went her way, and let us do the same.

Richard asked, "Why do you suppose no one ever told you about Aunt Edna and Caleb Wilkins?"

"Maybe it's just something nobody wanted to talk about. You know how the Burnettes are. We talk about each other all the time, but we don't really say a whole lot."

"'Full of sound and fury,'" Richard quoted, "'signifying nothing.' *Macbeth*, Act V, scene 5."

Frequently quoting the Bard is the closest my husband has to a fault, at least as far as I'm concerned. I was used to it, but my relatives still wonder how a Yankee who teaches Shakespeare at Boston College ended up in our family.

"Wouldn't it be great if we could find Caleb and bring him back home?" I said. "Wouldn't that be a wonderful present for Aunt Edna?"

"May I assume that you want to investigate this murder?"

"No, I'm not interested in the murder. I just want to find Caleb Wilkins." Richard looked suspicious, but I went on. "The question is, is he the kind of man I want in Aunt Edna's life? What if he really did kill Fannie Topper?"

"I thought you said he was found innocent."

"He was found not guilty, and that's not always the same thing. There just wasn't enough evidence to prove it beyond the shadow of a doubt."

"Aunt Edna is convinced."

"And look at Aunt Edna's late husband. He wasn't exactly a model citizen. No offense to her, but I want a little more to go on than her trust in her boyfriend."

"So you *do* want to solve the murder."

"No, I don't," I insisted. "I just want to make sure that it wasn't Wilkins."

"'The lady doth protest too much, methinks.' *Hamlet*, Act III, scene 2." I started to object, but Richard kept going. "How do you expect to get evidence of Wilkins's innocence without solving the crime?"

"I don't need evidence. I'll settle for an objective opinion."

"And which aunt, uncle, or cousin shall we consult for objectivity?"

"Not a cousin, because they're too young to know any details, same as me. And not an aunt or uncle, either. They all knew Wilkins, so they'd be biased, too. I think I'll talk to Chief Norton."

"Junior?" Richard said, meaning Byerly's current chief of police and a good friend of ours.

I shook my head. "Junior was just a kid when Fannie Topper was killed. I mean her father, Andy Norton." He would have been in charge then, and he had been as good at his job then as she was now.

I looked up the Nortons' phone number and dialed it. Chief Norton himself answered.

"Chief Norton? This is Laura Fleming."

"Well, hey there, Laurie Anne."

I didn't bother to correct him on my name; it wasn't worth it. Instead we chatted about life in Boston and folks in Byerly for a little while before I got down to business. "Chief Norton…"

"You better not call me 'Chief,'" he said with a smile in his voice. "Junior wouldn't like that. You can call me Andy."

"All right," I said, but I knew I wouldn't. In Boston I call people of all ages by their first names, but I just can't do it when I'm in Byerly. "The reason I'm calling is to ask you if you remember when Fannie Topper was killed."

"Laurie Anne, do you think there's been so many murders in Byerly that I'd forget one? Especially a case that was never closed."

"I guess not."

"What are you asking about Fannie Topper for, anyway? That was twenty–five years ago."

"My Aunt Edna got a Christmas card from Caleb Wilkins, and I want to find him."

There was a pause. "Edna never did believe that Caleb Wilkins killed Fannie."

"Do you?"

"That's not an easy question to answer." Another pause. "Laurie Anne, my wife has gone Christmas shopping with the girls. Why don't you and your husband come on over here and we'll talk about it."

❧

Chief Norton must have been watching for us, because he had the front door open before we got to the porch. "Come on inside," he said cheerfully. "It's colder than a polar bear's behind out there." He wasn't a tall man, but he had that same sense of presence that helped make his daughter a formidable police chief. His hair was all gray now, and he was dressed in slacks and a cardigan instead of the trim uniform he used to wear when I was young.

I introduced Richard, and once we got our coats hung up, Chief Norton led the way into the kitchen. Though I knew from previous visits that Mrs. Norton usually kept her kitchen spotless, this time every bit of counter was covered with sheets of decorated sugar cookies.

"Sorry there's such a mess. Daisy got all the cookie sheets ready so I can stick them in when the timer goes off." He grinned. "It was either do this or go along with her and the girls to carry bags. Sit yourselves down and I'll fix us some coffee."

We took seats around the kitchen table, cluttered with cookie supplies, and accepted the steaming mugs. "It smells heavenly in here," I said. It wasn't quite a hint, but I do love fresh sugar cookies.

Chief Norton held out a plate of broken cookies. "Help yourself. Daisy said I could have any that broke." He grinned again. "It's amazing how clumsy I can get if I work at it."

We spent a minute or two munching and complimenting cookies before Chief Norton asked, "Now what do you want to know about Fannie Topper's murder?"

I explained my idea for a Christmas gift, and finished with, "I know Aunt Edna thought that Wilkins was innocent, but before I track him down, I want to hear the facts from somebody else."

"Don't you believe your aunt?"

I didn't want to admit to somebody who wasn't family that I didn't trust Aunt Edna's judgment, so I said, "It's not that I don't believe her, it's just that after what happened with Loman, the last thing Aunt Edna needs is to be hurt again."

Chief Norton nodded, and I guessed I had given him the right answer. "Given what Junior has told me about your poking around in this murder and that, I might have guessed that you'd go after this one some day. What do you know about the case?"

"I know part of it just from hearing about it when I was young, but I don't really know the details."

Chief Norton settled himself down in that way that told me that a long story was coming, so I took another cookie and put on my best listening expression. Not only was it more polite, but you hear the most interesting stories that way.

"Fannie's Place was the most popular bar around Byerly at that time. Oh, there were fancier places, but hers was the best place to go to have a few beers and maybe a plate of barbeque. Fannie was just a little thing, and to see her, you'd never have thought she could run a bar like that. Always a smile on her face, and as nice as she could be, but she was as tough as they come. She made it a good place for people to go and have some fun.

"It was late summer, and the Walters Mill baseball team had just won the mill championship. Big Bill Walters was so tickled at having something to brag on that he threw a party down at Fannie's the day they won. He paid for a couple of kegs and the barbeque, even came by himself to shake the boys' hands. He hinted that there might be a little something extra in their pay packets that week, but of course after what happened, he wasn't about to pay no bonuses.

"The party went on into the wee hours. I was there myself for part of it, and it was a good time. Loud and rambunctious, but not rowdy. Fannie didn't let things get rowdy. Her brother Eb watched out for her, and he was the biggest man in Marley. Plus she had a shotgun behind the bar if people didn't want to listen to Eb.

"Caleb Wilkins was on the team, and he and Edna were there, dancing up a storm."

I found it hard to think of Aunt Edna dancing. Then I remembered what Aunt Nora had said about her.

Chief Norton went on. "As you might expect, the bar was one mess in this world after the party ended, so Caleb and Edna and a few others stayed on for a little while to help Fannie sweep up and take out the trash. I don't imagine they were much help, as high as they were, and Fannie finally chased them out, saying that she could get more done by herself. They all left at the same time, about two in the morning.

"Caleb took your aunt home, and your grandfather said they got there at about two–twenty and stayed out in Caleb's car for about twenty minutes before he turned on the outside light to let them know it was time for Edna to come inside."

I remembered Paw doing the same thing with me.

"For the rest of the story," Chief Norton said, "all we have is Caleb's word to go on. He said that he was on his way home when he realized that he didn't have his baseball cap. He figured he must have left it at Fannie's Place, so he turned around to go after it."

Chief Norton shook his head. "I asked him why he didn't just wait until the next day, and he said that he wished he had. It's just that he was a bit drunk and so happy about winning the championship that he didn't want to take a chance of losing that hat.

"Anyway, he said he got back to Fannie's at around three in the morning. He figured Fannie would still be up cleaning, and sure enough, the front door was unlocked. When he got inside, he saw that the place was a wreck, with the tables moved and everything pulled off of the shelves behind the bar. Then he saw Fannie lying on the floor in a pool of her own blood. He said he tried to revive her, but she was already gone. Supposedly that's why he had blood all over him when Fannie's boy Tim came in and saw them. Tim took one look and went running for help. He brought back his uncle Eb and Eb's wife, and they held the shotgun on Caleb while they waited for me to get there."

"It sounds pretty circumstantial to me," I said.

"It was circumstantial, all right, but the circumstances all fit the theory. Everybody in town knew that Caleb was saving up money to buy himself a house before he proposed to Edna, and everybody knew that Fannie was supposed to have a bunch of money stashed somewhere in the bar. The idea was that Caleb came back to look for it, and when Fannie caught him and threatened to call the police, he lost control and hit her. It looked like an accident to me. He pushed her or maybe punched her, and she fell and struck her head on the corner of the bar. He'd probably have gotten a light sentence if he had plea bargained."

"But he didn't."

Chief Norton shook his head. "He denied it to the bitter end. Enough of the jurors believed him that he was found not guilty."

"What do you think?"

Chief Norton didn't answer right off, just reached for another cookie and took his time eating it. "I always liked Caleb Wilkins, but he had been drinking that night. And he was in an awful hurry to marry Edna. I didn't want to believe that he was guilty, and when the court said he wasn't, I was willing to treat him that way."

I could tell that there was more to it. "But...?"

"Laurie Anne, there's nothing I can grab onto, but it just seemed to me that Caleb wasn't telling the whole story. At first I believed him, but after a while I got the feeling that he was holding something back." He shook his head regretfully. "I tried to get him to tell me what it was, but he just kept saying that he had told me everything he was going to."

"You don't have any idea of what he wasn't telling you?"

"I can't even be sure that there was anything, but I had this feeling."

Chief Norton's "feelings" were legendary in Byerly, so I took him seriously.

"That's all I've got," he said.

I asked, "Did you check on the other people who were at the party that night?"

"Of course I did."

"And?"

"A few of them had alibis, but most of them didn't. Pretty much everybody said they had gone home to bed. Either their wives and husbands verified it, which didn't mean a whole lot, or they went home alone."

"So somebody else who was at the party could have done it. Or somebody completely different."

"There weren't any strangers seen, and only people in town would have known about the money." He shrugged. "Now you know about as much as I do. What do *you* think?"

"I'm just not sure," I said honestly. I wanted to believe Aunt Edna and Aunt Nora, but the evidence was awfully compelling. Even so, Chief Norton hadn't been convinced Wilkins was guilty, despite the evidence, so maybe I shouldn't be either. "I guess that when we find Wilkins," I said, looking at Richard for confirmation, "we'll make up our minds then."

Richard nodded, and added, "If we can find him, that is."

"Finding him is no problem," Chief Norton said with a grin. "He owns a grocery store in Greensboro."

"How did you know that?" I said.

"I keep in touch with the police over there, have been ever since Caleb left Byerly."

"Why?" I asked.

"Fannie's money. We don't know that he found it because it wasn't on him, but we never found it anywhere else. I just wanted to see if he suddenly started spending more than he should have."

Richard said, "But he had already been tried once. You couldn't have arrested him again."

"Probably not," Chief Norton agreed. "Of course we only tried him for the murder, so we might could have tried him for the robbery if he started spending Fannie's money. At least, that's what I told the police in Greensboro. That wasn't the real reason. I just wanted to know. There were a couple of other murders while I was police chief that weren't officially closed, but I had a pretty good idea of who committed them. I never was sure of what happened to Fannie, and it kind of stuck in my craw. It still does, even after all these years." He drank the last of his coffee and said, "If y'all will wait for a minute, I'll go find Caleb's address for you."

Mrs. Norton and Junior's sisters arrived just as Chief Norton gave us the address, and after a few minutes of chatting, Richard and I took it as an excuse to leave. The last thing we heard on our way out the door was Mrs. Norton fussing at Chief Norton. "You made them eat broken cookies with all these nice ones fixed? What on earth were you thinking of?"

It was too late in the day to drive to Greensboro, so Richard and I headed back to Aunt Nora's for dinner. She wasn't really expecting us, but she knew we were in town and that meant that she'd cook about twice as much food as usual, just in case we showed up. I wasn't about to let any of her good cooking go to waste, especially not her biscuits.

This time I didn't mention Caleb Wilkins. Aunt Nora isn't the best woman in Byerly to keep a secret, and I wanted to be sure that Wilkins was worth bringing home before the word got out.

Instead we talked about the family: whether I knew that Sue was pregnant again and how Arthur was doing as city councilor and did I think that Ilene was serious about her new boyfriend. After all, that's why I come home for Christmas.

The next morning, Richard and I got up bright and early to make the two-hour drive to Greensboro. Since Wilkins owned a grocery store, our plan was to go to the store and see if we could spot him there. If we didn't get a chance to talk to him at the store, we'd go to his home address.

We got to Greensboro at around eleven and after consulting a map, found the store pretty quickly. It was a small place, but the number of cars in the parking lot showed that Wilkins had his share of customers.

I pulled out a shopping cart as we walked in the door.

"What's that for?" Richard asked.

"We can't just browse in a grocery store," I said. "It would look funny." We glanced around, but didn't see anybody old enough to be Caleb Wilkins, so we started slowly going down the aisles.

The shopping cart really had just been for camouflage, but I did find a few things to put inside.

"Pork rinds?" Richard asked, with a look of distaste.

"I like them," I said. And the country ham would keep for us to carry back to Boston, and you can't get Cheerwine, my favorite cherry soda, anywhere but in North Carolina. Fortunately, before I could fill the cart, we saw an older man with a name tag on that said, "Mr. Wilkins."

"There he is," I whispered.

"Looks decent enough."

Not like a murderer, Richard meant. I know you can't tell a book by its cover, but I certainly wouldn't have picked out the round–faced man with salt–and–pepper hair as anybody sinister.

I suddenly realized that this whole trip might be a waste of time if he were already married. Just because Aunt Edna was lonely didn't mean that he was. I took a closer look, and was relieved to see that there was no wedding band on his finger.

We were trying to be surreptitious, but I guess he could tell that we were watching him, because after approving a check for one of the cashiers, he came over to Richard and me.

"Can I help y'all with something?" he asked with a smile.

I said, "Mr. Wilkins? Mr. Caleb Wilkins?"

"Yes."

"From Byerly?"

The smile seemed to freeze. "I used to live there, yes."

"Mr. Wilkins, my name is Laura Fleming, and I'm from Byerly. This is my husband Richard."

There was a pause as we all tried to decide whether or not handshakes were appropriate. Good manners won out, and we briefly clasped.

"What can I do for you, Mrs. Fleming?"

"My aunt is Edna Randolph." Then I corrected myself. "Edna Burnette Randolph."

He nodded and looked a little more at ease. "The Christmas card I sent."

"Yes, sir. Do you think we could talk for a few minutes?"

He glanced around the store. "I think I could leave for a little while, and my house is just around the corner. Why don't we go there?"

We agreed, though I did wonder if going to a suspected murderer's house was a good idea. He spoke to his assistant while Richard and I paid for our groceries and loaded them into the car. Then we all walked to Wilkins's house. None of us spoke along the way.

Wilkins had a nice house, and I realized it was oddly similar to Aunt Edna's. It was just as neat, just as well–tended, just as empty. He let us into the living room, offered us a drink, and when we declined, gestured us toward the couch and sat opposite us in a wing chair.

Wilkins said, "I thought that it might be a mistake to send Edna that card. It's just that I was thinking of her and I wanted her to know. Is she doing all right?"

"She's fine."

"And the rest of your family?"

"Just fine."

"I remember that Edna's sister Alice had a little girl named Laurie Anne. Is that you?"

"Yes, sir." Then I added, "My mother passed away many years ago."

"I knew about that. I did try to keep up with things in Byerly for a while, but I haven't heard anything in a long time." He thought for a minute. "How's Edna's family? I know that she married Loman Randolph. They just had the one son, didn't they?"

I nodded. "Linwood. He's married himself now, with three children and another on the way."

"Is that right? I can't imagine Edna as a grandmother. She and Loman must be very proud."

"Actually, Loman has been dead for about a year and a half."

"I'm sorry to hear that. I didn't know."

I asked, "How about you? Did you ever get married?" It was probably rude to ask, but I had to be sure. I was pretty sure he hadn't, both because there was no ring on his finger and because the house didn't show any signs of a woman.

He shook his head slowly. "No, I never did." Wilkins went on to ask a few more questions about people in Byerly, and I answered them as best I could. Finally he asked, "Did Edna have a message for me or anything?"

"Not exactly," I said, feeling awkward. "Mr. Wilkins, we'd like you to come back to Byerly."

"Did Edna send you?"

"Not exactly," I said again, which was a polite way of saying not at all. "I thought that seeing you would be a nice surprise for her, sort of a Christmas present."

He leaned back, closed his eyes, and took a deep breath. I couldn't even guess at what he was thinking. Then he opened his eyes again and said, "I don't think that would be possible."

"I know about Fannie Topper, Mr. Wilkins," I said, "but it's been over twenty years. And you were acquitted."

"Edna must have told you how people in Byerly acted. I don't think that they've forgotten."

"But if you were innocent..?"

He smiled sadly. "That's what I mean. You're Edna's niece, and you're not even sure, are you? That's why I can't go back to Byerly. I've made a life for myself, and I'm happy enough. Nobody here knows anything about my past, so I don't have to worry about people whispering behind my back."

This wasn't what I had expected. I had thought that he'd want to renew his lost romance, that he'd jump at the chance to come home. I briefly considered bringing Aunt Edna to him, but then I thought about how angry she had been when he left. After all of that, I just knew she wouldn't come to him. The Burnettes have a lot of pride, and a lot of stubbornness. I know, because I'm as stubborn as a mule myself, which was why I wasn't ready to give up.

I said, "What if the real murderer was found? Would you come back then?"

"I don't think that's very likely."

"But if he was?"

He looked at me funny, but he said, "I suppose I might."

I looked at Richard, and he nodded slightly. "My husband and I have had some success in investigations before, and we've been looking into the case."

"Are you two private detectives, something like that?"

"We've worked with the police in the past, both in an official and unofficial capacity." Richard's face showed the strain, but he didn't say anything. Before Wilkins could press for any more details, I said, "Do you think you could answer some questions for us?"

He agreed, and I asked him what had happened that night. What he said didn't add anything to what Chief Norton had told us, other than a list of the other men on the championship ball team. Richard dutifully jotted the names on a pad he produced from his pocket.

After Wilkins had gone through the story, he said, "That's pretty much what I told Chief Norton all those years ago, and it didn't help him."

As delicately as I could, I said, "Chief Norton said he always thought you were holding something back. Is that true?"

He didn't answer for a long time, and I wondered if he was about to throw Richard and me out. Finally he said, "There was something, but it probably doesn't mean anything."

I just sat and waited, hoping that he'd go on.

"I never told anybody, not even Edna," he said slowly. Then he took a deep breath, and I guess he had convinced himself. "You know that when I went back to Fannie's Place, I was looking for my ball cap."

"Yes, sir."

"Well, that hat was the first thing I saw when I came in. It was lying on the floor next to Fannie's body. With blood on it. Chief Norton took it as evidence."

I nodded.

"A week or so later, after they let me out on bail, I dropped my keys onto the floor of my car and I had to reach up under the seat to get them. I found my hat under there."

I cocked my head. "If your hat was under there, then whose hat was it at Fannie's?"

"I don't know."

"So it must have been left by one of the other players." I didn't see why this was important.

"You don't understand. That hat wasn't there when I left the bar after the party. Edna and I stayed to help Fannie clean up, even swept up for her, and I know it wasn't there when we left."

"And the team members were the only ones with hats like that," I said, starting to get more interested.

Wilkins nodded.

"Couldn't somebody else have had one?" Richard asked.

"There weren't any more. Big Bill Walters would only pay for enough for the team members. If he had had his way, he'd have only had enough made for the fellows on the field at one time and made us trade back and forth. We talked him out of that idea, but you can be darned sure that he didn't get any extras."

"So what you're saying is that one of the other team members killed Fannie," I said.

"I'm not saying anything of the kind. All I'm saying is that the hat on the floor at Fannie's Place wasn't mine."

"Why didn't you tell Chief Norton? Maybe he could have found out who it was that was missing his hat."

Wilkins shrugged, and wouldn't quite meet my eyes.

"Was it loyalty? Did you think that it would be a bad thing to turn in a team member?"

He shrugged again.

"How could you be loyal to a murderer? The murderer didn't care anything about you. You could have been sent to prison."

"But I wasn't. If one of them killed Fannie, I know that he'd have come forward if I had been found guilty."

"He let you get chased out of Byerly without speaking up."

Wilkins was shaking his head. "You don't understand how it was. Every one of the fellows came to see me in jail. They raised the money for my bail, and they paid for my lawyer, too. How could I go to Chief Norton and tell him that one of those men was a killer? It would have looked like I was trying to save myself by dragging them down."

"Of course you realize that one of those men only helped out because he felt guilty," I pointed out.

"But the others did it because they were my friends," he shot back. "Chief Norton would have questioned all of them, stuck his nose into all kinds of places where it didn't belong."

I suppose I should have left it alone, but I just couldn't. "So you let a murderer go free?"

"I don't think it *was* murder. Even Chief Norton said it looked like whoever it was didn't mean to kill Fannie."

"What about Tim Topper? Don't you think he deserves to know what really happened to his mother?"

Wilkins looked down. "I felt bad about Tim, I really did. He was a good boy. But I couldn't bring his mama back no matter what I did."

"What about afterward, when the people in Byerly treated you so badly? Why didn't you tell Chief Norton about the hat then?"

"I thought about it, but that's all I did. I felt like I had made my decision and I'd have to live with it."

"What about Aunt Edna?"

Again he wouldn't meet my eyes. "In a way, Edna is the reason I had to leave Byerly. I could have stood it if it had just been me people were talking about. But I couldn't put Edna through that. She deserved better."

What I thought was that what Aunt Edna deserved was a chance to make her own choices, not have them made for her. I wanted to tell him that, too, but he looked so sad that I just couldn't. "Aunt Edna still cares for you," I said softly.

"I care for her, too."

Richard touched my shoulder then to tell me that it was time to go.

I had to make myself drive slowly on the way back to Byerly because I was so mad that I wanted to drive like a Boston cabbie. "Can you believe that man?" I demanded of Richard. "If Wilkins had told Chief Norton the truth all those years ago, the real murderer would have been found out instead of getting away with it, and Aunt Edna would have married him instead of Loman. She'd be happy now!"

"Don't you think you're laying an awful lot of blame on poor Caleb?" Richard said mildly.

"No, I don't," I said, but I didn't really believe it. I just couldn't stop thinking about how things might have been. "All right, I don't really blame Wilkins for everything that's happened, but I do think he should have told Aunt Edna what he was going to do. Aunt Nora said that she'd have gone with him."

"He didn't want to drag her down with him. He was trying to do the honorable thing."

"Honor!" I snorted.

"Since when is honor so distasteful? 'Mine honor is my life, both grow in one; take honor from me, and my life is done.' *Richard II*, Act I, scene 1."

"And they did take Richard's life away from him, didn't they?" Before he could respond, I said, "Do you remember Robert E. Lee?"

"The patron saint of the South?"

"Not to me! You know he was against secession? He was even asked to head up the Union army before he took over the Confederate forces. The only reason he fought for the South was his honor."

"This makes him a villain?"

"In a way it does. You know that the Confederacy never had much of a chance. They just didn't have the infrastructure they needed. The war should have been over almost before it started. But Lee was a genius. With him in charge, the war dragged on and on. How many people died for Lee's honor?"

"Aren't you simplifying it a bit?"

I ignored him. "Then there's Reconstruction. If the war hadn't lasted so long, the North wouldn't have been so hard on the South. Lincoln would have been alive well into the process and made sure of it."

"Unless Booth decided to attend an earlier show at Ford's Theater." I started to object, but Richard raised his hand. "All right, I'll concede that honor isn't always the best motive. But you can't play this kind of guessing game after the fact. Unless you're watching *It's a Wonderful Life*, that is." He looked at me suspiciously. "Which you watched last week, if I recall correctly."

I had to grin. "Actually, I watched it twice."

"Aha!"

As usual, Richard had dispersed my foul mood. "Well, since we don't have an angel to call upon to go back, we'll just have to go forward."

"Agreed, but first I want to remind you that I told you that this would happen."

"You don't mind, do you? Spending your Christmas vacation tracking down a murderer?" I could easily have added, "again."

"'At Christmas I no more desire a rose than wish a snow in May's new-fangled mirth; but like of each thing that in season grows.' *Love's Labour's Lost*, Act I, scene 1."

It took me a minute to worry the meaning out of the quote. "Are you implying that murder and trips to Byerly go hand in hand?" He opened his mouth to speak and I could tell that another quote was coming. "All right, you have a point."

"Then I think I'm entitled to one I–told–you–so."

I sighed. "I suppose you're right. Go ahead."

He shook his head. "No, I think I'll save it for later. When you're not expecting it."

"That's mean."

He grinned. "So now that you've bowed to the inevitable, what shall we do next?"

I thought for a minute. "How many men did Wilkins say were on the baseball team?"

He pulled out the list and counted. "'So Judas did to Christ: but he, in twelve, found truth in all but one.' *King Richard II*, Act IV, scene 1."

"So we have twelve men to track down."

"Actually only eleven. Wilkins himself is one of the twelve, but the quote was so obvious that I had to use it."

"Of course," I said, though I couldn't imagine how it could have been *that* obvious. "Maybe we should talk to Chief Norton again and see if any of them had alibis. I'd hate having to do the groundwork again, especially after all this time. Eleven men are a lot. Although if they're still working at the mill, they should be pretty easy to find." So many members of my family worked at Walters Mill that it would just be a matter of picking one to ask for help. "As soon as we get back, we'll give Chief Norton a call."

⋯⋯

We were nearly back to Byerly when I thought of something else. "Richard, are you hungry?"

"Planning to tackle some of those pig rinds."

"That's pork rinds. Or pork skins, if you prefer."

"I don't prefer either."

"Good. That leaves more for me. I wasn't suggesting them anyway. I was suggesting that we go to Pigwick's."

"I beg your pardon?"

"Pigwick's Barbeque. That's the name of Fannie Topper's old place. It might be helpful to scope the place out."

"It's still open?"

"Yes and no. They closed the bar after Fannie died, but her brother and sister–in–law kept the barbeque part going, just for take–out. Fannie's son Tim took over after a while, and I guess it was doing well enough that he decided to try it as a restaurant. So he opened Pigwick's a few years ago."

"Do I dare ask about the name?"

"From Dickens, of course."

"Of course."

"The napkins even have 'Pigwick Papers' printed on them."

"Of course." Richard was quiet for the rest of the drive, and I had a feeling that he was just glad that nobody had decided to honor Shakespeare in the way that Tim Topper had honored Charles Dickens.

It was mid–afternoon when we pulled into the parking lot at Pigwick's, which explained why there weren't many other cars there.

"Have you eaten here before?" Richard asked as we walked to the door.

"I've eaten their food before, but only take–out."

He raised one eyebrow. "Afraid of the ghost?"

"Not hardly. At least four Burnettes have died in Aunt Maggie's house, and you know that never bothered me." The reason was a different specter, one that still haunted Byerly. Marley was the "black" part of town. Getting food to take home was one thing, but actually going there to eat was something else. I felt a rush of liberal smugness that I was going inside, admittedly tempered by knowing how long it had taken to get me there.

The only other customers were a party of three men and a woman, all dressed in business suits. A big man with dark hair and caramel–colored skin was at the register by the door, and I recognized him as Tim Topper.

"Two for dinner?" he asked, picking up two menus.

"Yes, please," I said.

"We must be early," Richard said as Tim took us to a table.

"Just a bit," Tim said. "I expect the place will be filling up later." He handed me my menu, started to give Richard his, and then looked back at me. "Do I know you?"

"I think we've met once or twice. I'm Laura Fleming."

He shook his head, not recognizing the name.

"Laurie Anne Burnette," I said in resignation.

"That's right, now I remember. We talked at your cousin's victory party when he was elected to the town council."

I nodded. "This is my husband, Richard."

They shook hands and Richard said, "I take it you're an admirer of Dickens."

Tim grinned and shook his head. "No, that was my mama. She used to read me stories from Dickens when I was little, and the names were so funny that I used to get them mixed up. I could have sworn that she was saying Pigwick, and I thought that it would be a good name for a barbeque house." He took our orders, managing to talk us into getting large plates of pulled pork barbeque instead of the small ones we originally asked for.

As soon as he was out of earshot, Richard asked, "Aren't you going to ask about his mother's murder?"

I wrinkled my nose. "I don't think so. He was only ten when it happened, and I'm sure that Chief Norton must have questioned him pretty thoroughly. Besides, I can't just ask him about something like that out of the blue."

"You're not going to tell him that we're looking for the murderer?"

"If we find him, we can tell Tim then. I don't want to go dredging up memories like that, especially not at Christmas. It must have been awful for him, finding his mother dead like that."

"And this is where it happened?" Richard said, looking around the room.

I nodded, reminding myself that I didn't believe in ghosts. "Of course it probably looked a lot different." From what Chief Norton had said about Fannie's Place, I don't think it would have had big picture windows and gingham curtains and tablecloths. The floor would probably have been wood or tile, not carpet. The fireplace looked old enough to be original, but there was no sign of where the bar had been.

"And they never found Fannie's money?"

I shook my head. "Every once in a while, some of the kids would plan to sneak over here at night to search for it, but I don't think anybody ever did. Either afraid of the ghost or afraid of Tim's Uncle Eb. They just talked about how great it would be to find the money. Hidden treasure holds a certain appeal, doesn't it?" I looked at him, and from the gleam in his eye, I could tell that it certainly held a lot of appeal for him. "Richard, don't tell me that you want to look for the money."

"Just speculating."

"A lot of people have looked for that money over the years."

"True," he said.

"Of course," I added, "none of them were as brilliant as you are."

Richard grinned. "Is that so?"

We were turning around in our chairs to look for likely hiding places when Tim came back with our order. "Don't tell me that you're looking for my mama's money?" he said.

I didn't know what to say. It did seem pretty tacky. "I'm sorry—we didn't mean to be rude."

He held up one hand. "Hey, don't apologize. If you can come up with a place I haven't already looked, I want to hear about it."

Richard said, "If you don't mind my asking, why did your mother keep her money here? Why not in a bank?"

"For one, we didn't have a car so getting to the bank would have been a problem. For another, Big Bill Walters was still running the bank then and Mama just didn't trust him."

I could believe that. I didn't think that Big Bill was actively dishonest, but he was smart enough to think up ways that he could be honest and still get his hands on other people's money.

"She never told anybody where the money was?" I asked.

Tim just shook his head again, like he had been asked the same questions many times before. "You've got to remember, I was only a kid then. If I had known where it was, I'd have been into it every time I wanted a new toy."

"What about the people who worked for her?"

"There wasn't nobody but her, my Uncle Eb, and Aunt Fezzy. She wouldn't tell Uncle Eb because he'd been known to drink more than he should, and she wouldn't tell Aunt Fezzy because she might have told Uncle Eb. I know it sounds funny now, but things were different then. Mama was alone, and she had to think about the future. She had her heart set on my going to college, so she wanted to be sure that the money would be there for me."

For a minute he looked over toward the center of the room, and I hoped he was remembering his mother in life, not in death.

"I'm sorry," I said again. "We *are* being rude."

"Don't you worry about that. I imagine a lot of people have come in here because of curiosity. Maybe I should have called the place The Curiosity Shop." He grinned, and left us to our meal.

"I wish he wasn't so nice," I said to Richard. "I feel like such a heel."

"He said he didn't mind. And don't forget that we're doing this to find the person who killed his mother."

I nodded in agreement, but I still felt like a heel. Tim must think that we were like those people who slow down on the highway when passing a wreck. My parents had died in a car accident, and I had always hated the idea of people staring at them.

I didn't much feel like eating, but I took a bite of the bar-beque anyway. And another. And another. "You know," I said to Richard, "people might come here because of curiosity, but they come back for the food."

As Tim had predicted, the restaurant started to fill up soon after that, so we didn't have a chance to talk to him further other than to compliment the barbecue on our way out.

✿

When we got back to Aunt Maggie's house, I headed straight for the telephone.

"Hello?" Chief Norton said.

"Hi, this is Laura Fleming."

"I was hoping that you'd call. Did you go see Caleb Wilkins?"

"Yes, sir. We sure did."

"Did you find anything out?"

"As a matter of fact, he told us what it was that he wouldn't tell you."

"Is that so? Well don't leave me hanging."

I explained about the baseball hat, and why Wilkins never told him.

"Well I'll be darned. It never occurred to me that it wasn't his hat. I appreciate his loyalty to the other fellows, but it sure would have helped if he had told me the truth."

"I know. You don't happen to remember if any of the other ball players were missing alibis, do you?"

"It just so happens I dug up my files after we talked yesterday. I had a hunch that I'd want them. Have you got a pencil?"

I made gestures at Richard, and he handed me a pad and pen. "Go ahead."

While I waited, Chief Norton looked up each of the other eleven members of the team to check their alibis. As it turned out, two of them had ended up at a different party, five had gone to work the late shift at the mill, and one was seen to arrive at his home by a nosy neighbor.

"That leaves three," I said. "Joe Bowley, Pete Fredericks, and Bobby Plummer."

"That's what it sounds like to me, too," Chief Norton said. "None of them have ever been in any serious trouble, but then again, neither had Caleb Wilkins."

"They shouldn't be hard to track down."

"I expect not, but you do realize that by rights we should hand this new evidence over to Junior and let her deal with it."

"That's true." I should have been glad to let Junior take over. As long as it was solved, did it really matter who did the solving? But like I said, the Burnettes are stubborn. I was bound and determined to do this for Aunt Edna. Besides, Caleb Wilkins had trusted me. I wanted to finish it myself.

"Of course," Chief Norton said, "Junior's awfully busy this time of year. I hear that she's had a lot of trouble with shoplifting."

"Really?"

"This being such an old case, she probably wouldn't have a chance to get to it for a while. Until after Christmas, at least. And she hates it when I stick my nose in, so I can't do a thing."

"You're not suggesting that I withhold evidence, are you?" I said in mock surprise.

"Of course not," he said, in equally mock reaction. "In fact, you can let me tell Junior, just as soon as I get a chance.

You and your husband go ahead and do whatever you usually do on vacation. Now if you should happen to hear anything interesting, you be sure and let me know."

"I certainly will."

"Well?" Richard asked when I hung up.

"He's going to let us take a crack at it," I said. "If we can't figure it out by Christmas, Junior can take over."

"That gives us what? Three days?"

"Three days, and three suspects."

"But no motive other than this cache of money." Richard thought for a minute. "Laura, who was Tim's father?"

"I don't think Fannie was married, but if she was, he wasn't around anymore. Why?"

"It occurred to me that Tim has fairly light skin."

"Are you thinking that his father was white?"

"It's a possibility, isn't it?"

"I suppose, but I don't know how dark Fannie was."

"Wouldn't that have been a terrible thing to have happen in North Carolina? Didn't people around here look down on mixed relationships?"

"Mixed relationships were looked down on in most parts of the country!"

"Sorry. You're right."

I nodded, somewhat mollified.

Richard said, "The point I was trying to make was that Fannie might have threatened to make the father's identity public."

"Blackmail? I don't think she'd do that. Chief Norton seemed to think a lot of Fannie, and he's an awfully good judge of character."

"But she did want to send Tim to college. Maybe she asked the father for money, and he refused. She could have gotten mad and made the threat, or maybe he misconstrued what she said as a threat. Remember, Chief Norton didn't think the murder was premeditated."

"True. I suppose that one of our three suspects could be Tim's father." Then I thought of a complication. "So why the search for Fannie's money?"

"Maybe he wanted it to look like a robbery. Or even better, maybe Fannie had some proof that he was the father, and he was looking for that."

"It's possible," I admitted. "I was planning to talk to Aunt Nora to get some background on our three suspects, so I could ask her about that, too."

"You mean you don't already know all of the suspects? Angels and ministers of grace defend us!"

"Cut that out! I don't know *everybody* in Byerly." I looked questioningly at him. "*MacBeth*?"

"*Hamlet*. Act I, scene 4."

"I was close." Before he could argue the point, I said, "Shall we go talk to Aunt Nora?"

"We could, but if we go over there now, she's going to try to feed us and I'm still stuffed from the barbeque."

"Me, too." I checked the clock. "They've probably already eaten, but I'll use the phone this time. Just in case she's got leftovers."

After a few minutes of preliminaries, including my fending off an offer of Uncle Buddy coming by to deliver food, I said, "Aunt Nora, I need to pick your brain."

"Still trying to come up with a gift for Edna?"

I avoided answering directly by saying, "Richard and I

went to Pigwick's Barbeque today, and we were wondering about Tim Topper. Who was his father?"

There was a long pause. "Does this have something to do with Caleb Wilkins?"

So much for my surprise. "Yes, ma'am." I explained what Richard and I were trying to do. "Do you think it's a good idea?"

"Laurie Anne, that is the sweetest thing I've ever heard of." Darned if she didn't start sniffing.

"Well, I don't know if it's going to work yet," I said, feeling embarrassed.

"I know you'll do it, Laurie Anne. I just know it. Now what was it you wanted to know?"

"Tim Topper's father?" I prompted her.

"I'm sorry, Laurie Anne, but I don't have any idea."

I was surprised. "There must have been talk at the time. I mean, her not being married and all."

"Of course there was, but she never would say. I hear that when the doctor asked her what to put on the birth certificate, Fannie just said, 'His daddy doesn't want him, and I do, so you can put me down as mama and daddy, because that's how it's going to be.'"

"Does Tim look like any of the fellows she dated?"

"Not to speak of. Now she spent some time with her aunt in Saw Mills the summer she got into the family way, so it might not even have been anybody from Byerly."

I wasn't sure if the next question would shock Aunt Nora or not, but I had to ask. "Were there any rumors about Tim's father being white?"

"I thought that's what you were getting at. Of course people wondered, on account of his coloring. She was right much darker. Of course, that happens sometimes. Anyway, is there anything else I can help you with?"

"There are three men I need to talk to: Pete Fredericks, Joe Bowley, and Bobby Plummer. Do you know them?"

"Just to speak to. Do you think that one of them killed Fannie?"

"Maybe." I explained why. "Do they all still work at the mill?"

"I believe so."

"Then maybe I could go talk to them up there. Do you think Thaddeous could get me in?" Uncle Buddy and Willis worked at the mill, too, but as quiet as Uncle Buddy was, he wouldn't be nearly as good at introducing me to the men, and Willis worked the night shift.

"I imagine he could. I'll ask." She moved her mouth from the phone, but I could still hear her as she called, "Thaddeous! Laurie Anne needs to do some detective work at the mill." I cringed. "Never you mind what it's about. Can you get her in to see some men?" She named them, and he said something I couldn't quite make out. "I didn't think of that. Let me check." She came back to the phone. "Laurie Anne? The mill's Christmas party is tomorrow night and Thaddeous says you can go with him. That way he can introduce you."

"Doesn't Thaddeous have a date?"

There was a small sigh. "I'm afraid not."

"Then I'd love to go."

After that, I asked her for background on the three men, and had to write like crazy for nearly half an hour to keep up with her. And this for men she said she barely knew.

She finally stopped to take a breath. "That's all I know."

"That's plenty," I said. The F.B.I. should have such detail.

We talked a bit longer after that, mostly about what I should wear to the party. Once I hung up, I explained the arrangements to Richard. "When I talk to them, I'll be looking for a family resemblance."

"Which you will no doubt be able to spot instantly."

"You're just jealous because I can see these things and you can't."

"Is that so?"

"It is."

"So tell me—do you think Rudolph looks more like Donner or Mrs. Donner?"

After that, I had no choice but to chase him through the house with a sofa pillow.

⚜

Thaddeous picked me up at seven o'clock the next evening, and after Richard kissed me and told Thaddeous not to keep me out too late, we headed for the party. It felt odd to get kissed before a date instead of after.

"You look real nice, Laurie Anne," Thaddeous said as he handed me into his pickup truck.

"Thank you," I said, smoothing down the skirt of my deep red velvet dress. "You look pretty sharp, too." It was a shame he didn't have a real date. Poor Thaddeous was tall and nice–looking, and like his mama, he always had a smile on his face. Despite that, he had the worst luck with women of any man I had ever met.

We pulled out of the driveway and Thaddeous asked, "What's Richard going to do with himself tonight?"

"He thought he'd go over to the mall in Hickory and do some last-minute shopping."

"He's a brave fellow. That place is a madhouse this time of year." There was a short pause. "Mama told me what you and Richard are up to. Is there anything I can do to help?"

"Just taking me to the party is a big help."

"I know you want to talk to those men, so I figured I'd point them out to you and maybe introduce you to them. Then I'll leave you alone so you can see what you can find out."

"That's perfect."

"Now I don't want to see you going out into any dark corners with them. If one of them did what you think he did, you don't have any business being alone with him. And if you get into any trouble, you holler. Mama and Daddy are going to be at the party, too, and so is Willis. So somebody is going to be watching you the whole time."

I suppose it wasn't very liberated, but they meant well, and Thaddeous's advice was good. "I'll be careful."

The party was being held in the Byerly High School gym, because there really wasn't anyplace else in Byerly big enough, but the decorations committee had outdone themselves in making it look nice. It was still early, so after Thaddeous and I checked our coats, we headed for the refreshments table. It wasn't long before Thaddeous said, "There's Joe Bowley now. Are you ready?"

"You bet." While we waited for Joe to fill his plate, I remembered what Aunt Nora had told me about him.

"Joe is Burt Walters's second-in-command, thanks to Joe's daddy," she had said. "Don't get me wrong—Joe's a right smart fellow, and he'd probably have that job even if his daddy wasn't Big Bill Walters's best friend. The Bowleys had some money, though not nearly as much as the Walters, and Joe's daddy made sure Joe went to the same college as Burt. Joe always was a good community man, but since his wife died, he's really thrown himself into charity work."

Joe turned out to be balding and plump, and shook my hand enthusiastically when Thaddeous introduced us. When my cousin then came up with an excuse to leave us alone, Joe seemed perfectly happy to keep me company.

"Now you live in Boston, don't you?" he asked.

"Yes, sir."

"Now don't you 'sir' me," he said, wagging his finger. "You'll make me feel old. Call me Joe. Everybody does."

"All right, Joe." I took a bite of baked ham while trying to figure out how I could move the conversation in the direction I wanted it to go. "They certainly laid out a nice spread."

"I bet you don't get good cooking like this up North."

"That's the truth." That gave me an idea. "It's the barbeque I really miss. There's a couple of places that sell barbeque, but it's more Texas–style than North Carolina–style."

"That's one reason I could never live up there. I don't know what I'd do without good barbeque and hush puppies."

"I just try to get as much as I can when I'm home." Now for the subtle part. "I ate over at Pigwick's the other day. Tim Topper's place." I watched him closely for a reaction.

"They fix some good barbeque," Joe admitted without blinking, "but I think I like Fork–in–the–Road a mite better."

I suppose I shouldn't have expected him to turn pale at the mention of Tim Topper, because surely he had heard him named any number of times in the past twenty–five years. I tried something a bit more direct. "My Aunt Nora says that the barbeque there was better when Fannie Topper was cooking it. She said Fannie had a real knack for it."

Maybe he winced a little at that, but really no more than anybody would when reminded of an old murder. Then he launched into a list of recommendations for other barbeque houses across North Carolina, from Bubba's Barbeque in Charlotte to Buck Overton's in Mt. Airy to the Barbeque Lodge in Raleigh.

I guess he could tell that I was losing interest, because he finally said, "I guess you can tell that I enjoy my food." He patted his stomach with a grin. "You'd never know that I was the star player of my baseball team in high school."

"Oh, it still shows," I lied politely.

"My daddy thought it was important to play sports. Teamwork and all that. He always said, 'Even if you can't be an athlete, be an athletic supporter.'"

It was an ancient joke, but I joined in when he chuckled.

Then I asked, "Didn't I hear you played for the mill, too? On the championship team?"

He puffed his chest out a bit. "One of the proudest moments of my life, winning that game. Nothing like playing sports to make friends. I still keep in touch with all those men." Then he looked down at his plate. "Well, most of them."

I knew he was talking about Caleb Wilkins, but then he said that after talking so much about good food, he had to go refill his plate.

Thaddeous came up to me once Joe was gone. "How's it going?"

"Not much yet." I looked around, and saw that the place had pretty much filled up. "Have you seen either of the other two?"

"I just saw Bobby Plummer over by the dance floor. Come on."

When Aunt Nora told me that Bobby Plummer was said to have lace on his underwear, I had to stifle giggles. I hadn't heard that particular euphemism for being gay in years. She had gone on to say, "He was married for a year or so, but after the divorce, he moved back in with his mama. Now that she's gone, he lives by himself. He goes down to Charlotte a lot on the weekends, and somebody I know swears he saw him in one of those gay bars, dressed in leather pants." Damning evidence to be sure, but I had to wonder what Aunt Nora's friend had been doing at that bar.

Bobby was one of the better–dressed men at the party, both because of the quality of his suit and because of the style with which he wore it. Unlike Joe, he had a full head of dark hair, and a trim build. Once again Thaddeous introduced me, and then remembered that he was needed elsewhere.

We chatted, but I couldn't help noticing that Bobby was tapping his feet to the music.

"They're playing good stuff," I said, intending to some-how lead this to the celebration party at Fannie's.

But then Bobby asked, "Would you like to dance?"

I said, "I'd love to," but added the warning, "I'm not very good."

He smiled and said, "I'm sure you're wonderful."

Soon enough, he learned that I hadn't been exaggerating, but he was good enough to make me look competent. Unfortunately, I had never been one of those people who could carry on a conversation while dancing, and from the way Bobby was going, he'd have been happy to keep dancing all night long.

Finally I said, "I think I need to catch my breath."

"Of course." He led me to a table. "Can I get you a drink?"

"That would be very nice," I said. It would also give me a chance to come up with an approach. By the time Bobby returned with two glasses of punch, I was ready for him.

"I think I've been a desk jockey too long," I said. "I just don't have your stamina. You must be active in sports."

"Sometimes," he said. "I prefer working out on my own. I have a NordicTrack in my basement."

"I thought I heard something about your playing baseball. I was talking to one of your teammates earlier. Joe Bowley."

"That was years ago," he said. "The year we won was the last time that any of us played for the mill."

"Really? Why is that?"

"You're too young to remember, but it was after our victory party that Fannie Topper was killed, and one of the team members was arrested for the murder. A fellow named Caleb Wilkins."

"Oh?" I said, hoping I sounded interested enough to make him keep talking, but not so interested as to make him suspicious.

"Big Bill Walters fired Caleb right after he was arrested,

saying that he couldn't keep a murder suspect on the pay-roll. We team members didn't think that was fair. After all, Caleb hadn't been convicted. We talked about quitting, but since we couldn't do that, we decided we'd at least quit the team. If Walters wouldn't stand by Caleb, we weren't going to play just so he could have a trophy."

"So you turned in your hats?" Maybe I could find out who hadn't returned his hat, the one who had lost it at Fannie's.

But Bobby's next words dashed that hope. "No, we burned them. We set a fire in a trash can on the parking lot during lunch and tossed in every single cap. Big Bill was furious, but there wasn't anything he could do. He couldn't fire all of us."

I had to grin, even if it had ruined my half–formed idea. Unless... "That's great. Whose idea was it to burn them?"

"Oh, I think we all agreed on it. It was the sixties, and the revolutionary spirit had struck, even in Byerly."

By now I had my breath back, and Bobby asked me to dance again. In other circumstances, I'd have been happy to, but I declined with thanks and went looking for Thaddeous.

Instead I found Aunt Nora. "Are you enjoying the party?" she asked in an obviously innocent tone of voice.

"I'm having a wonderful time."

Then Aunt Nora lowered her voice. "Have you talked to them all?"

"Two out of three. I still need to track down Pete Fredericks."

"You come with me, and we'll find him." Aunt Nora wasn't as efficient a guide as Thaddeous was because she had to stop and say hello to just about everybody we saw, but eventually we made our way over to a tall, thin man with short, graying hair and dark eyes. He was standing alone near the edge of the room, smoking a cigarette.

"Hey there, Pete," Aunt Nora said. "Pete, do you know my niece, Laurie Anne? She lives up in Boston."

We made the obligatory small talk about how different Massachusetts was from North Carolina. Then Aunt Nora excused herself to go powder her nose, leaving me alone with Pete.

I try not to have any illusions about my feminine charm, but from what Aunt Nora had told me about Pete, I was halfway expecting him to make a pass at me once we were alone.

She had said, "Pete has an eye for the ladies. I think he's gone out with every woman in town, or at least with any of them that would. He wanted to date Edna once, but she wasn't about to put up with his roving. He had to get married about fifteen years ago, but Martha knew what she was getting into and she seems pretty happy. He's probably still running around, but at least he's careful."

I had to wonder if he had dated Fannie Topper, but I could not for the life of me come up with a way to gently broach that subject. The best opening gambit I could devise was, "What do you do at the mill, Pete?"

"Supervisor of dying right now, but I gave notice just this week."

"Is that so? Are you going to work for a different mill?"

"No, I'm going to work with my wife's uncle. Maybe you know him. Harry Giles."

"Over at Giles Funeral Home?"

"I like to say that I'm moving from dying, to dying."
Darned if he didn't already have that solemn, restrained
smile down pat.

I suppose I should have been able to easily move the
conversation from death to a particular death, but I just
couldn't do it. I even asked about how they made bodies
presentable for open casket ceremonies, specifically when
the deceased had died by violence, but the answer was far
more graphic than I had wanted and left no room to ask
about Fannie Topper.

Trying to change the subject, I mentioned playing baseball, and he told me about a grisly case when his uncle had
a client who died from a blow to the head from a baseball.
I don't even want to think about what he told me when I
mentioned barbeque.

By the time Aunt Nora came to rescue me, I didn't know
whether or not Pete was the murderer, but I was pretty sure
that he wouldn't be fooling around on his wife any more.
Not if that was his idea of pillow talk.

The party went on for hours, but I could have left right after
talking to Pete Fredericks for all the good it did me. I hadn't
learned anything useful. Still, I didn't want to make Thaddeous miss the celebration, so I stuck around and tried to
have fun. I even danced with Bobby Plummer some more.

It was around one o'clock when Thaddeous and I finally
headed for the parking lot.

"Sorry I wasn't much of a date for you, Thaddeous," I
said.

"That's all right. Did you get what you were after?"

"Not really."

"Don't you worry. I know you'll puzzle it out."

I was glad somebody had confidence in me. At that point, I sure didn't.

We were all the way to Thaddeous's pickup before I saw the man leaning up against it.

"Richard!" I said. "What are you doing here?"

"Were you afraid I'd keep her out too late?" Thaddeous said with a grin.

"Just couldn't stand being away from her any longer," Richard said, and gave me a big hug.

Thaddeous snickered. "I suppose you're going to steal my date."

"You've got it."

I thanked Thaddeous again for his help, and got into the car with Richard while my cousin drove away.

"If you came to get me to find out what I learned, you wasted your trip," I said.

"That bad?"

"Just about." I told him everything I had learned from the three men, and concluded with, "I didn't get the first hint of a motive, unless Fannie was blackmailing Bobby Plummer because he's gay."

"Is he gay?"

"I don't even know *that* for sure."

"What about family resemblances? Could any of the three have been Tim's father?"

"He doesn't favor any of them. I had wondered if Pete could have been the sower of wild oats, but the way he is now, he'd be more interested in Fannie dead than alive." I threw my hands up. "It was a complete waste of time."

"Not complete. The part about the hats was significant. Burning them couldn't be coincidence. Now we're sure that the murderer was one of the team members."

"True," I said, "but we were pretty sure of that before."

Richard patted my leg comfortingly.

We drove a few minutes longer, and it dawned on me that we weren't headed for Aunt Maggie's house. "Richard, where are we going?"

"To Pigwick's."

"At this time of night? I imagine they're closed." Richard didn't answer. "What are you up to?"

"Nothing much," he said. "I just figured out where Fannie hid her money, that's all."

"You what? Where?"

He pulled a paperback book out of his jacket pocket. "The answer is in here."

I read the cover. "*Oliver Twist*?"

"Tim said that his mother loved Dickens, and I've read a little Dickens myself. Contrary to popular opinion, I do enjoy things other than Shakespeare. All that talk about Tim's father reminded me that Dickens used more than one case of disputed parentage or illegitimate birth. I thought I remembered something about a hiding place, too, so I went to the Waldenbooks at the mall and looked at Dickens books until I found what I was looking for."

I was impressed. Dickens wrote long books. "And?"

He handed me the book, and switched on the car's dome light. "I've got it marked."

There was a slip of paper sticking out near the end of

the book, and when I opened it, I saw that Richard had circled a passage. "You wrote in a book?"

"Desperate times call for desperate measures."

Clearly he thought this was important. I read the passage out loud. "'The papers,' said Fagin, drawing Oliver towards him, "are in a canvas bag, in a hole a little way up the chimney in the top front–room."' What papers?"

"The papers that proved who Oliver's parents were. And I remembered a fireplace at Pigwick's. Of course in Fannie's case, I'll bet the papers are green with numbers and presidential portraits on them."

"And maybe something that proves who Tim's father was?"

"That's what I'm hoping." He looked toward me, obviously expecting expressions of delight.

I didn't disappoint him. "Richard, you're brilliant!"

He tried to assume a modest expression. "Well, we should probably wait until we find out if I'm right or not." Still, he broke into a huge grin, like a cat who had just swallowed a particularly plump canary.

⚓

It was almost two in the morning, so we weren't surprised that Pigwick's was dark when we drove into the parking lot.

"Drive around back," I told Richard. "There must be a stairway up to Tim's place. I was right, and we climbed up to knock at the door. When that didn't work, we progressed to pounding with our fists.

Finally Tim opened the door, wearing a pair of jeans he must have just pulled on and rubbing his eyes. "What's going on?"

"Sorry to wake you up, Tim, but we think that Richard's figured out where your mother's money is.

That woke him up. "Are you serious?"

"Richard, read him that piece from *Oliver Twist*."

Richard complied.

I asked, "Is it possible?"

"Well, we sure never looked in there," Tim said. "I know Mama had read *Oliver Twist*, but she was only halfway through reading it to me when she died. I never had the heart to finish it." He stepped back from the door. "Come on in, and we'll go look."

Stopping only to put on a sweatshirt and pull a flashlight out of a drawer, Tim lead us through his apartment, down the stairs, through the kitchen, and into the dining room. He flipped on the lights and said, "I'll turn the heat up."

I guess it was cold in there, but I was too excited to notice. All I could do was stare at the brick fireplace that nearly filled one wall.

"Well," Tim said, "let's see what we can see."

All three of us started tugging on the bricks that made up the fireplace. We must have spent an hour, and I know that no brick escaped our attentions. Tim even pulled out a stepladder so he could get to the highest bricks.

"Did y'all find anything?" Tim finally asked.

I shook my head.

Richard pulled out *Oliver Twist* again and said, "The book says the money was on the inside of the chimney."

"Then let's try that." Tim got down on his hands and knees and hunted up inside, using the flashlight to light his way. Richard and I watched eagerly at first, but as the minutes passed, it was obvious that he wasn't finding anything. Finally he crawled back out. "Nothing!"

"Let me try," I said, reaching for the flashlight. I was both shorter and smaller around than Tim, so I could get a little further in. Not that it did me any good. All I found was soot. I knew I was ruining my coat and my dress, but I just didn't care. Finally Richard tugged on my foot, and I gave up and came away from the fireplace.

"I'm sorry, Tim," I said, feeling foolish. "We really thought this could be it. Here we got you out of bed and everything."

"No, that's all right. It sounded like a good idea to me, too. I don't really need the money anyway. Pigwick's is doing fine. I just thought if I could find it, maybe I could go to college part–time, and get that degree Mama wanted me to have."

Now I really felt awful for raising his hopes for nothing. "I'm sorry," I said again.

Tim looked at the clock. It was almost four. "I may as well stay up and get the meat ready to cook. I'm supposed to cater a lunch in Hickory today. Your car's in back isn't it? Come on out to the kitchen, and I'll let you out that way."

He didn't even wait for an answer before going into the kitchen.

Richard looked even more forlorn than Tim had. "It *was* a good idea," I said, and rubbed his back.

He said, "'The attempt and not the deed confounds us.' *MacBeth*, Act II, scene 2."

It was when I heard Tim rattling around in the kitchen that something rattled loose in my brain. I pulled at Richard's sleeve. "Hold on just one minute! You may have solved it after all!"

Tim had pulled out a big pan, and was opening the walk–in refrigerator. The kitchen was all stainless steel and tile. There was an oven, but it looked brand–new. Besides, it wasn't big enough to cook a whole hog in.

"Tim, you don't cook the barbeque in here, do you?"

"No, I've got a stone oven out in a shed. Mama said she had to put it out there or it would have been too hot in here in the summer."

"So it's the same one that your mother used?"

"Of course." Then he caught onto what I was talking about. "You don't suppose...?"

"Where's the shed?" Richard asked.

Again Tim led the way as we went outside, cut across the parking lot, and into a wooden shed that held a few shelves and a huge oven. I looked up at the stone chimney rising up from the oven, and saw Richard and Tim doing the same.

I asked, "Is it possible?"

Tim said, "The only thing is that we keep it going most of the time." Even at this hour, I could feel low heat rising from the oven. "I don't see how Mama could have put anything inside without burning herself."

I said, "What about on the outside?"

Richard went to one side and Tim to the other, and started pushing on the stones at eye level. After a few minutes, they shook their heads.

"Maybe it just needs to be pulled harder," Richard said. "It's been a long time."

"Maybe," Tim said doubtfully.

I said, "Tim, how tall was your mama?"

"About your height, maybe an inch or two shorter." He smiled, catching on. "We were looking too high up."

This time I squeezed in and started pushing and tugging. Long minutes went by, with Tim and Richard watching anxiously, and I think I would have given up if it hadn't been for the hopeful light in Tim's eyes. Even with that encouragement, I was just about ready to admit defeat when I felt a rock give a little. "That one moved," I said.

"Can you pull it out?" Richard asked.

I tried, but couldn't get a good grip.

"Let me," Tim said, and reached around me. I guess cooking ribs is better hand exercise than punching keys at a computer all day, because he had it pulled out in a second. Or maybe he just had a stronger motive than I did.

Once he had the rock out of the way, I stuck my hand into the hole and felt a piece of cloth. "There's something in here." I yanked and pulled out a canvas drawstring sack. It was about as big as my biggest pocketbook, and looked about half full. I was tempted to open it myself, but that wouldn't have been right. Instead I handed it to Tim.

He swallowed visibly as he pulled the string. It came partway loose, then disintegrated. "Rotted through," he said, and pulled on the bag itself. The canvas held for a second longer, then came open and Tim looked inside. A yell burst out from him, and he grabbed an enormous stew pot from on top of the stove and spilled the contents of the bag out into it.

Neatly banded parcels of bills poured into the pot.

"It's Mama's money!" He reached his arms around both me and Richard and clutched us to him in a bear hug.

The three of us danced around and did our best to

recreate the lost Rebel Yell. Eventually I remembered the other reason for our treasure hunt, and pulled myself free. "Is there anything else in there?"

Tim laughed, handed me a slotted spoon, and said, "Just stir it up and see!" Then he danced around some more with Richard.

I used the spoon to rummage around the bills. A couple of stacks came loose because the rubber bands containing them had given up, so I didn't find it right off. Besides, I was looking for papers or an envelope. What I found was a badly tarnished box.

"Tim, was this your mother's?" Not knowing how long fingerprints could last, I didn't touch it, just pointed with the spoon.

Tim finally stopped dancing. "What is it?"

"I think it's a cigarette case." I still had on my coat, so I reached into my pockets to find my gloves, and only picked it up after I had my hands covered.

Tim took a look. "I don't think so. Mama didn't smoke. And that looks like silver."

I flipped it open. It was filled with cigarettes, but they didn't look mass-produced. "I don't think these are tobacco."

Richard and Tim nodded.

"I know my Mama didn't smoke pot," Tim said firmly. "She didn't even like Uncle Eb drinking because she didn't want me picking it up."

"Maybe this was the reason she was killed," I said slowly. Possession of marijuana might be a misdemeanor now, but twenty-five years ago, it could have led to a long jail sentence. "What if the murderer was looking for this, not for the money?"

Tim looked confused, but then, he didn't know what Richard and I had been up to. "Caleb Wilkins was a junkie?"

"I don't think it was Caleb Wilkins," I said. "I'll explain it all later, but right now I think we ought to call the police. Maybe they can still find fingerprints on this, and figure out who it belonged to."

"We won't need fingerprints," Richard said. "Hold the case up to the light again."

I closed the case, and took a closer look at the front. The inscription was obscured by the tarnish, but after a minute I read the initials out loud. "JB."

❧

"Well, Joe," Andy Norton said. "Do you want to tell us what happened?" He hefted the cigarette case, now encased in a plastic bag.

Joe Bowley wasn't smiling now. His chubby face had gone slack, and he wasn't meeting Chief Norton's eyes.

It was around nine o'clock in the morning by then. Neither Richard or I had gone to bed after finding Fannie's cache. Instead we had called Junior Norton and her father to come take charge of the cigarette case, and told them all we knew. After that, we had all gone to the police station to wait until it was late enough that Junior could go get Joe Bowley.

Junior even deputized her father so he could lead the questioning, since it had been his case originally. "It's an early Christmas present," she had said with a grin. An odd present, maybe, but no more odd than what Richard and I were trying to give Aunt Edna.

Now Richard, Junior, Tim, and I were waiting for Joe's answer. He had already waived his right to have a lawyer present, and even agreed to let Tim, Richard, and me listen in.

Joe took a long, ragged breath, and started to speak. "I didn't even like pot much at first—that's the crazy thing. I only started smoking because some of the guys liked it, and I always carried it around in case somebody wanted to smoke with me. Nobody did at the party, but I went around back of the shed to smoke one anyway. To celebrate winning. That's where Fannie found me. Lord, she was mad. Said she didn't need drugs around her bar.

"I probably shouldn't have offered her one, because that just made her madder, and she snatched the case away from me. She said she wouldn't call the police, but I was going to have to tell my daddy or she would. She said she'd give him the case back when he came to talk to her.

"I was going to tell him, I was going to tell him that night. Only when I got home, he kept saying how proud he was of me for playing such a good game. I couldn't tell him then.

"So I went back to Fannie's late that night, after everybody else had gone home. I just wanted more time, but she said I had to tell Daddy right away. I offered her money to keep quiet, but she said that she was going to call Daddy the first thing in the morning." He shook his head, not so much in regret as in complete lack of understanding. "She just wouldn't listen to me."

"Is that when you hit her?" Chief Norton asked.

Joe looked shocked. "You make it sound like I meant to hurt her. What happened is that she wanted me to leave, and I wouldn't go without my case. She said she was going to get her shotgun, was even heading for the bar to go get it. I just wanted to stop her, so I tried to catch her arm. She wriggled away, so I had to grab her. She kept moving, trying to get away, and she pushed herself away from me and lost her balance. That's when she hit her head. It was an accident."

"If it was an accident," Chief Norton said quietly, "why didn't you call for help?"

"I didn't think she was dead—I thought she had just knocked herself out. I had to find my case. I knew it was there somewhere, and I didn't want anybody else to find it."

I wasn't supposed to talk, but I couldn't help asking. "What about the blood? Didn't you even check for a pulse?"

He didn't really answer me, just said, "I would have called for help once I found the case."

Chief Norton said, "Didn't you stop to think that if Fannie had been alive, she could have called your father when she woke up? Maybe even the police?"

"She wouldn't have done that, not without the case as proof. It would have been her word against mine, and Daddy wouldn't have believed a ni—" He looked at Tim and stopped. "She knew that."

"But you didn't find the case."

I pictured him ripping up the bar while Fannie lay there bleeding, and shivered. Richard took my hand.

Joe shook his head. "I looked everywhere, and then I heard a car drive up. I didn't know it was Caleb. I thought it was Fannie's brother, and he might have been drinking. He'd have killed me if he had found me in there with her like that. So I went out the back door and drove away."

"You must have thought that I'd come looking for you

pretty soon," Chief Norton said. "Why didn't you try to run?"

"I didn't have anywhere to go. This is my home, my family is here."

Byerly had been Caleb's home, too, I thought.

Joe went on. "The next day I heard about Fannie being dead and Caleb being arrested, but nobody mentioned my cigarette case. I was sure that Caleb would get out of it. He was innocent, after all."

I didn't find his trust in our legal system very touching.

Chief Norton said, "What about your hat?"

Joe looked surprised that he knew that part, but answered anyway. "I saw I didn't have mine a couple of days later, and that's when I thought about getting the team to burn them all as a protest. Like burning flags and bras the way people did then."

I didn't think that anybody had ever burned a bra to hide evidence of a murder.

Finally Joe met Chief Norton's eyes. "I did what I could for Caleb. We paid for his bail and his lawyer, never asked for a penny of it back. Walters would have hired him back eventually. He didn't have to leave town like that."

Easy for him to say when he hadn't been the outcast.

He looked down at his hands. "I tried to make up for it."

I remembered what Aunt Nora had said about Joe's charity work, and wondered how much of his life had been spent trying to make up for Fannie Topper. He had done everything but the right thing.

❧

"So Joe murdered Fannie," Aunt Nora said after Richard and I had told her about it.

"It wasn't murder after all," Richard said. "Joe told us it was an accident, and I believe him. Even Tim said he couldn't hate him."

I wasn't quite so forgiving as Richard and Tim, but I had to admit that Joe had looked right pitiful sitting there, knowing that he was finally going to have to tell his father the truth.

"Did Junior put him in jail?"

I shook my head. "She let him go home for now. She's not sure what the district attorney is going to want to do."

"Have you called Caleb?"

"First thing. I had to get Andy Norton on the line to convince him that it was true, but he said he's going to meet me and Richard at Aunt Maggie's on Christmas morning. Then we'll bring him over here." The Burnettes always gathered together on Christmas morning, and this year Aunt Nora was the hostess. "I can't wait to see Aunt Edna's face."

Then I thought of something. "Aunt Nora, do you suppose you could throw some hints around that Aunt Edna might want to dress up a bit?" After all this, I didn't want Caleb to be shocked by her appearance.

"I think I can handle that. Why don't you two go get yourselves some sleep. You look like you've been ridden hard and put away wet."

"That sounds like an excellent suggestion," Richard said, and pulled me out of the chair before I could fall asleep right where I was.

We slept most of that day to catch up, and since the next

day was Christmas Eve, we stayed busy wrapping gifts and visiting. Chief Norton brought over a platter of Christmas cookies, and Tim Topper delivered enough sealed bags of barbeque to feed my habit for a year.

Christmas morning dawned bright and clear. Richard and I were up early to exchange gifts before joining in on the official Burnette celebration. Then we ate breakfast with Aunt Maggie and sent her along to Aunt Nora's house so we could wait.

Caleb showed up right on time, dressed in what had to be a new suit, and grinning from ear to ear. He kept trying to thank us, but I finally got him into his car by telling him that we were going to be late.

The plan was for him to follow us, and let us go inside first. After a few minutes, he would ring the bell and we'd make sure that Aunt Edna answered.

Caleb looked nervous, but no more than I was. As we drove to Aunt Nora's, all of a sudden I was wondering if this had been a good idea. What right did I have to meddle this way? Aunt Nora had said that Aunt Edna had been furious at Caleb when he left. What if she didn't want to speak to him?

"It's going to be fine," Richard said. "Even if they don't get together again, I'm sure they'll enjoy seeing each other."

"What if they don't get along anymore? Aunt Edna has changed an awful lot." I kept remembering the picture of how she used to be. If that was the woman Caleb was expecting to see, he was going to be disappointed.

"It's going to be fine," Richard repeated. "Don't get your shorts in a bunch."

I had to giggle. "Where did you hear that?"

"Aunt Nora, of course. You didn't think *that* was Shakespeare, did you?"

Finally we were there. Richard and I parked on the street, and I made sure Caleb had parked behind us before we went inside.

The house was filled nearly to the bursting point with aunts, uncles, and cousins, and it took me a few minutes to spot Aunt Nora. I called her name, and she bustled over to me.

"Is he here?" she whispered.

"He's outside. Where's Aunt Edna?"

"Ruby Lee took her to freshen up. Here they come now."

I looked up that way, meaning to wish them a merry Christmas, but I never did get the words out.

Aunt Edna was wearing a dark red dress that flattered her slim figure, and matching pumps. Her hair had been released from its bun, and trimmed and curled around her face. She had on a pearl necklace and earrings, and even eye shadow and lipstick.

"Merry Christmas, Laurie Anne," she said, smiling shyly.

I looked at Aunt Nora, and she grinned. She and the other aunts must have spent the past two days re–making Aunt Edna.

Before I could say anything else, the doorbell rang. Aunt Nora must have prompted everybody, because even though there were several people near the door, nobody moved.

"Edna, would you get that?" Aunt Nora asked innocently.

Aunt Edna looked curious, but went to the door and opened it.

From over her shoulder, I could see Caleb holding a bouquet of roses and a wrapped box. "Hello, Edna," he said.

I held my breath for her answer.

"Caleb Wilkins," she said. "I was wondering if you'd ever show up again. What do you want?"

My heart went right through the floor. She *didn't* want to see him.

"I'm sorry, Edna," he said. "I've regretted leaving you like I did every day for the past twenty–five years."

"I hope you don't think I've been sitting around waiting for you to come back!"

"No, I didn't think that. I just hope you'll let me come back now."

"For how long this time?"

"Edna, I swear that the only way I'll leave again is if you want me to." He paused. "Are you telling me to go?"

They stood there for what seemed like an eternity, both so filled with pride that it hurt to watch them. Aunt Edna's head was held high in a way I had never seen before, and I finally understood why Aunt Nora had called her the one with spirit.

Finally Aunt Edna said, "No, I'm not telling to you to go, Caleb. I'm asking you to stay." She reached out a hand, and Caleb took it. Then suddenly she was out on the porch with him and they were in each others arms, kissing with twenty–five years' worth of passion.

After a few stunned seconds, Aunt Nora closed the door behind them and wiped her eyes.

Richard put his arms around me, and we kissed, too.

"Merry Christmas, Richard."

"Merry Christmas, Laura." Then in a voice loud enough for everybody to hear, he added, "God bless us every one!"

The Death of Erik the Redneck

This story features Junior Norton, the police chief in Byerly.

I'd known Erik Husey ever since we were in grammar
school, but when I looked at the smoking mess that had
been Erik and his dog, Lucky, all I could think of was that
I never thought he'd be that *dumb*. To go out in a rowboat
and set yourself on fire with a cigarette when you're so
drunk that you don't even *think* to jump into the water, is
just out–and–out stupid.

"Who found him?" I asked Mark Pope, my deputy. We
were both standing on the floating platform that served as
a dock for Walters Lake, looking down at Erik's body in his
boat.

"Wade Spivey. You want to talk to him, or shall I give you
the high points?"

"I may as well talk to him myself." I didn't doubt that
Mark had all the facts, but sometimes it helps to get the
story from the horse's mouth. Before I went over there, I
asked, "Did you call the medical examiner?"

"Right after I called you."

"How about Erik's wife?"

He shook his head.

Mark just can't stand breaking the news to the next of kin. It's a good thing it doesn't bother me so much. As the chief of police of Byerly, North Carolina, I can't avoid it. "I'll talk to her later."

I walked down the dock to where Wade was staying out of our way. "Hey, Wade. How're your folks doing?"

"They're fine, Junior."

"Glad to hear it."

"And your folks? How's your daddy liking retirement?"

My daddy was police chief before me, like his daddy had been before him. Which is why I'm named Junior, instead of the kind of name you'd expect for a woman. "He likes it pretty well." With manners attended to, I said, "Mark tells me it was you who found Erik Husey."

"That's right."

"Why don't you tell me about it?"

"Well, I saw his boat on the lake with smoke coming from it this morning."

"What time was that?"

He thought about it. "I slept late this morning so it must have been after ten before I came outside to get the paper."

Knowing Wade, that meant he had been out drinking the night before, but unlike Erik, he had had enough sense to stay off the lake. "And then you saw the smoke?"

"Well, it wasn't much smoke. Just a little curl coming up, like he was having a cigarette. Only I couldn't see him over there. I called out a couple of times, and when nobody answered, I got to thinking that something might be wrong, so I went to take a look."

"Was your boat handy?"

"Tied up at the dock like always. It didn't take me no time to go over there, and that's when I saw him."

"Not a pretty sight."

"It sure wasn't," he said, shaking his head. "Anyway, I tied a line to the bow and towed it in. Then I called you folks."

"Any idea of how long he'd been out there?"

"He wasn't there when I left for town yesterday evening, but I don't know about when I got back. It was dark last night, and I don't think I even looked in that direction."

"Didn't hear anything?"

Wade shook his head.

"Good enough. I appreciate you letting us know right away."

"No problem. Y'all want some coffee? I put a pot on right after I called."

"I sure would. Thank you."

Wade went into his trailer, and I went back over to Mark.

"Good thing his boat's aluminum," Mark said. "If it was wood, it would have burnt right through and sunk. There's no telling when we'd have found him."

I nodded, looking inside the boat again. Like I had said to Wade, it wasn't a pretty sight, and it didn't smell too good, either. Erik was lying flat on his back, with a bottle in his right hand. The label had been burned off, but the bottle looked like Rebel Yell whiskey, the cheapest brand I knew of. On his left side was what was left of Lucky, a brown and white mutt who had wagged his tail at everybody he met.

"Lucky must have passed out first," I said, "or he'd have tried to wake up Erik."

"Lucky was probably drunk, too," Mark said.

"Erik gave whiskey to his dog?"

Mark nodded.

"That man was dumber than—" A station wagon drove up before I could finish the insult. "Dr. Connelly's here. Why don't you get the Polaroid from my trunk and take a few pictures before he gets started?" I handed him the keys.

While he left, I took another look at Erik and Lucky. I've seen people dead from gun shots, blunt instruments, and way too many car wrecks. I was pretty sure that this was the first man I had seen die from stupidity.

Which is how I ended the story when I was telling it to my parents that afternoon over Sunday dinner. I suppose most people wouldn't have thought it a fit subject to speak about at the dinner table, but after all the years Daddy was a cop, he and Mama had heard it all.

"That must have been awful for you," Mama said.

"I've seen worse." Smelled worse, too, but not many times.

"But this time it was somebody you knew."

"Mama, I know most of the people who end up dead in Byerly." Byerly isn't that big.

"But Erik was your age. In your grade at school, wasn't he?"

I nodded.

"Doesn't that bother you?"

"It always bothers me when somebody dies in my town."

"That's not what I mean. Andy, you know what I mean, don't you?"

"What your mama means, Junior, is that she's surprised that you're not taking it more personal this time."

I took one last bite of pecan pie. "Can't say as I am,

Daddy. I didn't know Erik that well, and I didn't like him much. About the only time he ever spoke to me was to make fun of my name or to complain about speeding tickets."

Mama just sighed and tapped the maple dining room table. "Junior, I swear you haven't got a bit more feeling than this table here. What about Rinda? How did she take it?"

Rinda was Erik's wife. "About as well as you'd expect. She cried a little at first, but then wanted to know what happened. She hadn't been up long enough to worry about where Erik was. Said he'd gone out drinking the night before, and she figured he'd fallen asleep at somebody's house."

"Erik always did drink too much," Daddy said. Despite retirement, he kept up with most people in Byerly. "But I thought he drank at home. Cheaper that way."

"Rinda said he usually did, but they had had a fight."

Mama said, "That's terrible! The last words they spoke were in anger."

"Kind of suspicious, too," I said.

"Junior! It was an accident."

"Probably," I agreed. "She said they weren't fighting about anything important anyway, only about him not taking care of the house when she was out of town last week. She just got back from going to her father's funeral in Tennessee."

Mama said, "I heard about that. She hopped right onto a bus when she heard how bad off he was, but missed being able to say goodbye to him by an hour. It really hit her hard." She shook her head. "First her daddy, and now her husband. Junior, I've got a big dish of chicken and dumplings that I was going to freeze for later this week, but I want you to take it over to Rinda."

"Mama, I'm the police chief. I can't be taking food over every time somebody gets killed in an accident."

"I don't see why not. Especially when it's somebody you've known your whole life."

I looked at Daddy, hoping he'd be on my side, but he said, "I don't think it would hurt anything, Junior." Then he winked. "Besides, she might confess."

"Andy!"

So later Sunday afternoon, when I should have been cleaning up my apartment or doing nothing at all, I drove back to the lake and Rinda Husey's house. There were extra cars in the driveway, meaning that Rinda had company, so I wouldn't have to stay any longer than it would take to drop off the chicken and dumplings. At least, that's what I thought.

It wasn't Rinda who came to the door, it was Erik's aunt Mavis.

"Afternoon Miz Dermott. My mama wanted me to bring this over for Rinda." I held out the dish, but she didn't take it from me.

Instead she called out, "Mary Maude, did you call Junior?"

My mama tells me that Mavis Dermott and Mary Maude Foy had always had dark hair, but now they dye it solid black, without the first highlight to make it look real. Both wear face makeup so thick that it could be a mask, especially the way it ends right under their chins. Mavis is a widow, and since Mary Maude's husband is an invalid who never leaves the house, she might as well be one, too.

"No, I didn't call her, but I'm glad she's here," Mary Maude said. "Junior, I want you tell Rinda that it's not legal for her keep things that Erik inherited from his mama. Those things ought to come to me and Mavis."

Now I had to go inside. "Hello, Rinda," I said, ignoring Mary Maude for the time being. "My mama sent this for you."

Rinda looked a lot more tired than she had before, but with Mary Maude and Mavis pestering her, I wasn't surprised. She had been blonde and vaguely pretty when she and Erik started dating in high school, but between the marriage, a few extra pounds, and what she had been through, she didn't look pretty anymore. Even her blonde hair had grown out so that the dark roots were showing.

"Thank you, Junior." She took the dish from me and went out into the kitchen.

"Miz Foy, did Erik have a will?" I said.

"Of course not, him being so young. But I know he'd have wanted those things to come to me and Mavis."

"With no will, his property belongs to Rinda, and she can do with it as she sees fit."

"But it's not right," Mary Maude insisted.

"That's the law."

She muttered under her breath about law and police.

Mavis said, "Didn't I tell you that, sister?" To me, she added, "She didn't pay a bit more mind than the man in the moon. It's just a shame, that's all. Those things have been in our family for three generations."

I wanted to ask what things they were so worried about, but it didn't really matter and Rinda came back in then.

"Junior, do you know when I'll be able to claim Erik's body?" she asked.

"Dr. Connelly said he'd get to it just as quick as he could."

Mary Maude said, "That's another thing. Why can't we bring Erik home now? You've got no business cutting into him."

I guess Rinda had heard it before, because she didn't even wince. I said, "I'm sorry Miz Foy, but when a man is found dead under—" I started to say "suspicious," but changed it to keep from riling her up further. "Under unusual circumstances, there has to be an autopsy."

This gave Mary Maude a chance to mutter some more, and Mavis a chance to say, "Didn't I tell you that, sister? They'll fix him up for the funeral. Isn't that right, Junior?"

I hesitated. Usually Connelly does keep an autopsy as neat as he can, but in this case, the body had been pretty messy to start with.

Rinda came to my rescue. "He was burned to death. There's nothing an undertaker can do with that."

Just for a second, the aunts were struck silent. Then Mavis said, "Lord all mighty, Rinda, I didn't know you were so hard. Don't you have any feelings?"

That sounded darned close to what my mother had said to me, so I felt like I should defend Rinda. "She's right, ma'am. You wouldn't want to see him the way he is."

Both Mary Maude and Mavis started bawling, and I was impressed by the way their makeup repelled the tears. Rinda tossed a box of tissues at them, then walked me to the door. "Thank your mama for me, Junior."

"I will. Are you going to be all right with them two?"

"They'll quit as soon as they realize they don't have an audience." She didn't sound hard to me, just realistic.

I was getting into the car when Mark called me on the radio. "This is Junior."

"Junior, Dr. Connelly wants you to call him."

"Let me get to a phone." Mark gave me the number, and I started up the car. I could have gone back inside to use Rinda's phone, but I wanted to stay as far away from that house as I could. Besides, the only case Connelly was looking at was Erik's, and I wasn't about to discuss it in front of his family.

There was a filling station with a pay phone a mile down the road, so I pulled in there to call. "Dr. Connelly? This is Junior."

"Junior, I found something that might interest you."

"What's that?"

"When I examined Lucky's body—"

"Don't you mean Erik's body?"

"No, I mean Lucky's."

"You autopsied the dog?"

"I thought it would be interesting. I dissected cats and pigs in school, but never performed a post–mortem on a dog. That was all right, wasn't it?"

Different strokes for different folks, as Daddy says. "I don't see why not. What did you find?"

"A couple of things. First off, that dog's lungs were clear as a bell."

"Meaning what?" I asked, though I thought I knew the answer.

"Meaning that that dog never inhaled smoke from any fire."

"Which means that Lucky was dead before the fire started?"

"That would be my opinion."

"Then what killed him?"

"There's some fluid in the stomach, and it looks like anti-freeze. You know dogs love the taste of antifreeze, even if it is toxic."

I ran through a few possibilities in my head. First, maybe Erik accidentally left antifreeze out where Lucky could get it, and burned himself to death in a fit of remorse. Or maybe it was some sort of dog murder/suicide pact. Or maybe it was just plain old everyday murder. It seemed to me that the last idea was the most likely.

"You said a couple of things?"

"This may not be important, but Lucky had been oper-ated on in the past few weeks. He had a scar in the stomach area, healing nicely. Clearly done by a professional."

I didn't see how that mattered, but you never know. "What about Erik? How did he die?"

"I was just getting ready to start on him, but I thought you'd want to hear about the dog immediately."

"You thought right. Let me know what you find out about Erik." I hung up the phone, and got back in the car to radio Mark and tell him what Dr. Connelly had told me. "I guess you know what I want you to do."

He's not got much imagination, so he had to think about it. "Go talk to everybody living near the lake and see if they saw anything?"

"That's right."

"I'm on the way. How about you?"

"I'm going to see Wade Spivey again."

Actually, it wasn't Wade I wanted to see so much as it was his boat, but I thought I better check with him before I went sniffing around. He was watching a football game when I knocked, but invited me in anyway.

"Hey, Junior. Anything wrong?"

"A couple of odd things have shown up in the Husey case. You mind if I ask a couple more questions?"

"Not at all. You want a Coca-Cola?"

"No, thank you." Drinking coffee with someone who found an accident victim was one thing. Drinking a Coke with the first man on the scene of a murder was something else. "Did you know Erik well?"

"Just enough to speak to."

"But he docked his boat right next to yours."

"Only because he bought the boat from Ralph Stewart. Ralph had always kept it there, so I said Erik could just keep on leaving it there."

"So y'all never went fishing together?"

"Erik wasn't a real fisherman. He'd throw out a few lines, but mainly he just went out there to be by himself."

"Did you ever know anybody to go out on the lake with him?"

"Just his dog. I shouldn't say this after what happened to him, but I used to think Erik would only bring Lucky because of him being so tight-fisted. He'd have had to share his Rebel Yell with a human being."

"He was a careful man with his money," I said, but knowing how Wade drank, I couldn't blame Erik for not wanting to share. "But didn't he give whiskey to Lucky?"

"He used to," Wade said, "but the vet put a stop to it. She told him that Lucky was going to die from cirrhosis of the liver if he didn't stop. And Erik thought the world of that dog."

I was glad to hear that Erik had had some sense after all. Though Lucky would have been better off with the whiskey than the antifreeze. "Now you leave your boat out there at the dock so anybody could come use it if they wanted to."

"I suppose so. Do you think somebody did?"

"I don't know. Do you mind if I have look at it?"

"Not at all. You want me to come with you?"

"No, you enjoy your football game. I've messed up enough of your day."

I knew darned well he was going to be watching me through the window instead of the game, but I wanted to look around on my own.

Wade's boat wasn't much of a much. It had a motor, and enough room in it for two or three people. Maybe more, if one of them was dead. I squatted on the dock, looking down into the boat. No blood, but there was some light-colored hair or fur caught on the bench. Wade's hair was brown, but Erik's had been dirty blond and Lucky's brown and white.

I had some evidence bags in my pocket, so I put the hair into one of them. I thought about dusting for prints, but decided it wasn't worth the effort. Wade's boat was made of wood, not the best surface for prints, and everybody knows to wear gloves these days.

I gave the boat another look, this time getting in and looking under things, but didn't find anything more incriminating than a package of fish hooks, so I went back to my car. Wade was trying to hide behind a curtain, so I pretended not to see him.

I radioed Mark, getting him as he was driving to the next

person on his circuit of the lake. I told him I'd start on the other direction, and we'd meet in the middle.

Neither of us got anything. Walters Lake isn't that big or that scenic, and not many people live right on the water. Wade's place was the closest, and Erik's own house the next after that. Nobody saw or heard anything.

There was another dock on the other side, but the only boat there was leaky and I don't think even a murderer would take a chance on taking it out at night.

"So what have we got?" Mark asked when we met.

It seemed right obvious to me, but Mark likes to have things spelled out. "It looks like somebody brought the bodies out here, arranged them in Erik's boat, used Wade's boat to tow Erik's boat out to the middle of the lake, set it on fire, then left Wade's boat where he found it."

"Had to be a local to know where the boat was, and that Wade wouldn't be home."

"I don't think Erik had many enemies from out of town. Or Lucky either." I looked at him sidewise to see if he'd noticed he was being made fun of. He hadn't. "But I want to talk to Dr. Connelly before I do anything else. Why don't you head back to the station, and I'll call and see if he's finished with Erik's autopsy." I found another pay phone, reminding myself to ask the city council for a couple of cellular phones in the next year's budget.

I guess he wasn't done yet, because it took a while for him to answer the phone, and when he did, he said, "Dr. Connelly," in a tone of voice that meant that I had interrupted him.

I decided not to ask about the autopsy right off. "Dr. Connelly, this is Junior. I've got a sample of hair or fur I found in Wade Spivey's boat. Can you tell me if it matches either Erik or his dog?"

This must have interested him, because he sounded less cranky when he spoke again. "I'm not sure. I can tell if it's human or canine, and if it's human, I can tell you if it matches Husey. But I don't know if I can get a positive identification on a dog. I'd have to do some research."

"Should I run the sample up to you?" Byerly didn't have its own coroner. Connelly served the whole county, and he was a good thirty minutes away.

"It's getting late. Why don't you call the vet in town. He can tell you if it's dog or not, and maybe he knows if you can ID canine hair."

"I'll do that." Now to butter him up. "Do you think you'll have the autopsy on Husey done by the first part of the week?"

"First part of the week?" he said, sounding pleased with himself. "I should have preliminary results this evening."

I whistled in appreciation, some of it sincere. "That's fast work." If I had asked him to have it done that night, he'd have fussed. "Will you call the station when you're done?"

"Of course."

I hung up the phone, grinning a little. And Mama said I didn't have feelings. Of course, I had to admit, I hadn't treated Dr. Connelly like that to make him feel better so much as to get what I wanted.

I was out of quarters, so I drove on over to the veterinarian's place. Josie Gilpin, who insisted everybody call her Dr. Josie, was an older woman with no family who spent most of her weekends tending to animals who were too sick to go home. I didn't think she'd mind a little company and from her smile when she opened her door, I was right.

"What can I do for you, Junior? You didn't find another dog hit by a car, did you?"

"Not this time. I was wondering if you could take a look at a sample of hair I've got and tell me what it came from."

"I can try. Come on in." She led me through a room where the floor was strewn with dog toys and the furniture covered with dogs. They were well-trained and didn't even bark as we walked through and down a hall to where Dr. Josie had a lab set up, complete with microscope, test tubes, and such.

"What animal do you think it came from?" she asked.

"Either human or dog," I said, handing her the evidence bag. "I want to see if it came from Erik Husey or his dog Lucky."

"I heard about them two," she said, which didn't surprise me. News travels fast in Byerly. "Erik should have had more sense, risking Lucky's life like that."

Dr. Josie is partial to animals, and I guess that's why she lives alone. She used tweezers to pull part of the fur out and put it on a slide. Then she turned on the microscope, put in the slide, and peered at it.

"Lucky had been operated on recently," I said. "Was that your work?"

"Sure was. Erik brought Lucky in a few weeks ago, said he was acting puny, not eating."

"Was it from the drinking?"

"Did you know about that? You know, Junior, there are laws about mistreating animals."

I held up both hands in surrender. "I only heard about it

this morning, or I'd have said something to him. Anyway, I hear you did a good job of laying down the law yourself."

"You bet I did. But it wasn't the whiskey that made Lucky sick. He had a blockage in his intestines. I had to operate."

"Is that how you found out about the drinking, when you had him cut open?"

She was still peering, so I couldn't see her grin, but I could tell that she was. "As a matter of fact, I didn't see the first sign of it. It's just that I had heard that Erik was giving that dog whiskey, and knew if I scared him, he'd stop."

For an animal doctor, she was pretty smart about people. Then I said, "I'm surprised Erik paid for an operation like that, him being so close with his money."

"He didn't even argue with me. Paid half up front, and the rest in payments. He may have been cheap, but not when it came to Lucky." She pulled the slide out of the microscope. "Well, it's not dog, cat, horse, or squirrel."

"Human?"

Dr. Josie shrugged, no longer caring, and handed me the evidence bag. "Probably."

"I appreciate your help." She showed me out past the dogs, and I went to the station to see if Dr. Connelly had called.

He had, and what he'd told Mark caught me by surprise. Erik really *had* died in the fire. Only thing was, he had been hit in the head beforehand, hard enough to knock him out. Dr. Connelly said that he might not have lived even without the fire.

"What do you think?" Mark said after he made his report, letting me draw any conclusions there were to be drawn.

"I might be able to convince myself that Erik got so

drunk that he fell and hit himself on an oar or something. The fire could have wiped out any trace of that. But there's two things that bother me."

"What two things?"

"One, Lucky already being dead. And two, the hair I found in Wade's boat."

"So how do you make it out?"

I sighed, wishing he could put one and one together without my help. "Somebody killed him."

He nodded like I had confirmed something rather than giving him the whole idea. "Who do you think it was?"

"We'll start with the obvious suspects. Rinda, of course." The spouse is always the first one you look at. "She said they had a fight Saturday night."

"Would she have told you that if she killed him?"

"Maybe she thought the neighbors heard yelling. And I want to look at those aunts of his. They were fussing about something they wanted and how Rinda wasn't going to let them have it. Maybe it's valuable. And I guess I have to consider Wade Spivey. It wouldn't be the first time that the killer was the one to 'find' a body."

The only other person I could think of was Dr. Josie, and I didn't think even she'd burn a man alive for giving whiskey to a dog. And she'd never have hurt Lucky.

I looked at the clock. "It's too late to start anything now. I'll see you tomorrow." Mark frequently slept at the station, one ear listening for the phone. I did it too, when I had to, but preferred my own apartment.

I guess Mama would have been put out if she had found out how I slept when someone I knew had been murdered, but I slept like a baby. Not even a bad dream.

Dr. Connelly had told Mark he had a couple of early appointments, and I should wait until eleven or so before calling. So I spent the morning making phone calls.

First I called Erik's insurance agent. There's only two agents in town, and I guessed the right one the first time. He was the cheaper of the two, and of course, Erik's life insurance had been the cheapest available. There was just enough money to bury Erik if Rinda didn't mind a pine box.

Then I called Mary Maude Foy to find out just what it was that Rinda was keeping from her and Mavis. I made it sound like I was seriously investigating their claim, and she was mad enough at Rinda to believe it. The thing was, it turned out to be nothing more than a double bed, a dresser, and a chest of drawers. Mary Maude and Mavis were strange, but I didn't think they'd kill their own nephew for a bedroom set. I did make a note to ask Rinda if that's all they were asking for, and to call Maggie Burnette, a dealer at the local flea market who could tell me if the pieces were worth anything.

Then I headed for Dr. Connelly's with the sample of hair. Other than the drive, the visit didn't take long. Dr. Josie had already told me that it wasn't Lucky's fur; it turned out that it wasn't Erik's hair either. Which I should have known, since Erik and the dog had been in Erik's boat, not Wade's. Dr. Connelly showed me something that told me who it was in that boat.

Now I knew who, but I spent the drive back to Byerly trying to figure out why. Mama had said that I didn't have any feelings, but the person who killed Erik must have had feelings, strong ones. To burn a man to death would take an awful lot of feeling. Not to mention killing his dog. It took me most of the drive to figure out just why the killer had hated Erik that much.

I radioed Mark as I got into Byerly so he could make a phone call for me, and had just got out to the circle of houses around the lake when he called me with the answer I needed. Then I told him to come out there and meet me, in case there was trouble.

There was only one car in the driveway at Rinda's house this time, and she answered the door herself. "Hey, Junior," she said. "What can I do for you?"

"I wanted to let you know that the doctor's finished Erik's autopsy," I said. "He'll be able to release the body today."

"I'll be glad to get the funeral taken care of."

"I know you will be. One thing I wanted to ask you. How did you find out about the vet bill?"

Her face turned white as a sheet, much whiter than her hair. "The vet bill?"

Her reaction was enough for me. "Rinda, I have to arrest you for the murder of Erik Husey. Before I go any further, let me read you your rights." I did so, put the cuffs on her, and walked her out to my squad car just as Mark showed up to escort us to the station.

"She killed him over a vet bill?" Mama asked that night over dinner. We don't eat together every night, but I knew Daddy would want to hear the whole story. Mama, too, even if she wouldn't admit it.

I said, "It wasn't just the money. Rinda said she had always known that Erik was cheap, and she accepted that. So when her daddy was dying and he said they couldn't afford for her to fly to Tennessee, she didn't argue. You know she only missed being able to say good-bye to him by an hour—she'd have made it if she had taken a plane. Then when she got back, she found the last vet bill, and it showed how much Erik had paid for Lucky's operation."

"So she killed the dog to keep him from barking while she killed Erik for revenge," Daddy said.

"Nope. Rinda said she never intended to kill Erik, and I believe her. She just wanted to kill Lucky. She left a bowl of antifreeze out for him that morning. Only he didn't die right away like she thought he would. Dr. Josie says that it takes twelve to twenty-four hours for a dog to succumb to antifreeze poisoning. Rinda watched that dog all day long, waiting for him to die."

Mama shivered a little, and I didn't blame her.

I went on. "The later it got, the more desperate Rinda got, so she finally gave him some more and that did it. She was meaning to put the bowl away before Erik got home, but he left work early. When he found Lucky dead next to the bowl, he knew Rinda had done it on purpose."

"So he came after her and she was only defending her-self," Daddy said.

"Yes and no. He was carrying on pretty bad, and said he was going to kill her. When he took a swing at her, she picked up a skillet and hit him."

"Cast iron?" Mama asked.

I nodded.

"So she thought he was dead when she burned him," Mama said.

"No, she knew he was still breathing. She wanted him dead."

Daddy said, "Did she think he'd come after her again when he woke up?"

"I asked her that, but she said she wasn't a bit scared. She was mad. Mad about not being able to say goodbye to her daddy, and mad about him spending money on a dog, and maddest of all about him wanting to murder her over that dog. She was determined to kill him. Now she thought that if she burned him, we wouldn't be able to tell he'd been hit in the head. She was going to put him in the car and run it off the road, but she wasn't sure it would catch fire. Besides, she said, it was the only car they had. The boat she didn't care about, so she put Erik and Lucky in a wheelbarrow and pushed them over to the lake. She knew Wade would be out drinking, so she borrowed his boat to tow with. She wasn't sure how she caught her hair on the boat." I had known it was hers as soon as Dr. Connelly told me the sample was bleached blonde. "She used whiskey to start the fire, actually stayed and watched. Said she had to make sure he didn't wake up." It made me right sick to my stomach to think about it. "And you said *I* don't have any feelings."

"I didn't mean that, Junior, and you know it," Mama said. "I just don't want you to forget that it's people you're working with, not cases."

I nodded. She might have a point.

"What happens now?" Mama asked.

"I think Rinda will plead guilty, but even if she doesn't, it should be open and shut," I said.

"What about Erik's funeral?"

"His aunts are going to take care of it. Spending their own money to do it, too, because Rinda won't let them have the insurance money. Maybe they aren't so bad after all. And they'll get that bedroom set."

"All over but the paperwork," Daddy said. "Nice job, Junior."

"One other thing," Mama said. "You said Rinda didn't resist arrest. So how did you get that dirt on your uniform?"

I looked down at the dark patches on my knees. "Well, Dr. Connelly called and said the funeral home had come after Erik, but he didn't know what to do with Lucky. Rinda said we could throw him on the trash heap for all she cared, but I just couldn't see it. So I took him over to Dr. Josie's place and buried him there. She's got a little cemetery for dogs and cats."

Darned if Mama didn't tear up. "That's the sweetest thing I've ever heard. And I said you didn't have any feelings."

With her crying, I knew I had feelings all right, but what I felt most was embarrassed.

An Unmentionable Crime

This story features Sue, who is married to Laura Fleming's cousin Linwood.

✺

If Sue had been anywhere else, talking to anybody else, she'd have said, "Now don't get your panties in a bunch," but she knew Ida would fire her on the spot if she dared say such a thing to Annabelle Lamar while working at Petticoat Junction. Especially when it was her salmon pink panties that Miz Lamar was mad about.

Miz Lamar's nostrils were flaring, her eyes were flashing, and she was doing all the other things folks do when they're too highfalutin to cuss.

"Were there or were there not panties sent with my ensemble?" she asked.

Sue shrugged, and looked pointedly at Ida. She was the manager—let her take the heat.

"Well..." Sue could see that Ida wanted to blame the supplier, but Miz Phelps, Tori Dupont, and Tori's daughter Marie had been watching when she opened the box, and they'd seen her hang up the panties along with the bra, camisole, and garter belt. Lee Fredericks had come in later, but he'd seen the complete set, too. So, naturally, Ida got out of it by passing the buck to the only other person around.

"Sue," she said sternly, "I told you to keep an eye on things while I was helping Miz Phelps. What happened to Miz Lamar's undergarments?"

Ida had said no such thing, but Sue wasn't willing to lose her job over saying so. "I don't know, Ida. I was helping Tori and Marie, like you said to."

"She helped me, too," Lee said, which was nice of him.

Unfortunately, Miz Lamar wasn't so nice. "Are you saying that anybody off the street could have taken my panties?"

"Of course not," Ida said. "Nobody's been in here except—" She stopped, but it was too late. The only people who could have taken those drawers were right there in the store. In other words, Ida herself, Miz Phelps, Tori, Marie, and Lee. And Sue. It didn't take a whole lot of smarts for Sue to figure out which one Ida would rather blame.

"Call the police," Miz Lamar said. "I prepaid for this ensemble, and I insist on having it complete."

"I'm sure we have another pair of panties in stock that will go with the set," Ida said.

"Don't be ridiculous," Miz Lamar snapped. "The color, the trim—they're unique."

Sue had to admit that Miz Lamar had a point. There really wasn't anything in the store that would work, and no place else in town carried anything like it. There might be something close in the mall in Hickory, but Sue was willing to bet that it wouldn't be an exact match.

Ida swallowed hard but managed to get out, "Then I'll refund your money."

"Unacceptable! I ordered the set to wear to the cotillion tonight, and I will accept nothing less. Call the police."

The other customers were getting irate, and Sue didn't blame them. Miz Lamar had as good as accused one of them of stealing her panties. What did she think the police were going to do? Strip search everybody? Miz Phelps looked indignant, Tori was holding onto her daughter protectively, and Marie was mortified. As for Lee, he was sweating bullets. Sue didn't have any idea that he had stolen anything, but he did have a secret, and it might come out if the police got involved.

"Sue," Ida said in a strangled voice, half begging her to come up with something, half warning her that her job was on the line if she didn't.

Getting the police involved was a sure way of losing some of their best customers; even if one of them really was a thief, it would be awfully bad for business. And if Petticoat Junction closed, Sue could kiss her new minivan goodbye.

The day had started out bad and gotten worse. First off, Amber was teething and wouldn't stop whining. And Crystal snagged Sue's pantyhose while she was chasing Jason, which meant that she'd had to dig up another pair. Then Tiffany announced that she wasn't speaking to her because Sue wouldn't buy her a bra. If all that weren't enough, Ida had been on her back from the minute she got to work.

"Sue, have you seen the mailman?" Ida said.

"Not yet," Sue answered for the umpteenth time.

"Fiddlesticks!" Ida said. That was the closest thing to

cussing Ida would allow herself at work. She wouldn't let Sue cuss either, but Sue had decided she'd rather say nothing as to say *fiddlesticks*.

Sue turned back to her customer, and said flatly, "You go ahead and buy that bra if you want, Miz Phelps, but I'm telling you, it ain't up to the job."

Mary Jacobs Phelps, who was anything but flat, glared at her. "I like a feminine bra."

"Suit yourself, but if you get that bra, your boo—" Sue stopped herself just in time. Words like *boobs*, *hooters*, and *butt* were also forbidden at Petticoat Junction. "Your breasts are going to hang halfway to your knees. At your age, they don't stand up on their own."

"I'll have you know that my breasts are as firm as they were the day I got married."

Sue was willing to believe her, but before she could say so, she saw Ida in the mirror, hovering behind them. Ida raised her eyebrows at Sue in a clear message. So Sue said, "Is that right? Well, that's nice, that's real nice."

Miz Phelps looked suspicious, but went back to admiring herself in the mirror.

Sue was tempted to let her go ahead and buy that pitiful excuse for a bra, even though she knew it would be stretched out of shape in no time.

The only thing was, if she did, Miz Phelps would come back and squawk that they'd sold her inferior merchandise, and Ida would blame Sue for it. So she was going to have to be tactful, even though tact wasn't her strong suit.

Sue smiled the way she'd seen her husband's cousin Vasti smile when she was sucking up to somebody. "You know, Miz Phelps, since you are so firm and all, I should show you the Le Bustier 3000. It emphasizes the bust line a lot more than that bra, and it would be a shame not to show off a figure like yours." Actually, Miz Phelps had a figure like a tugboat.

Ida was still hovering, so Sue decided to lay it on even thicker. "We don't stock many of the model I'm thinking of, because most women aren't big— Aren't well enough endowed to carry it off. You wait here and I'll get you one out of the storeroom."

While Miz Phelps simpered, Sue went in back and got the Le Bustier Model 3000, which they kept out of sight because it was so huge nobody would admit to needing it. She pulled off the size tag, and started to replace it with a tag with the size Miz Phelps thought she took. Then she had an inspiration and replaced it with a tag for one size smaller than that.

Sure enough, Miz Phelps checked the tag as soon as Sue handed it to her. She looked doubtful, but was all smiles when she opened the slatted door to the dressing room and said, "It fits!" in a tone of amazement. "Of course, it's not as pretty as the other one—"

"Maybe it's not as low cut," Sue said quickly, "but it seems to me that men want women to leave a little something to the imagination." She smiled the Vasti smile again, and held her breath while Miz Phelps thought it over.

"I believe you're right," she finally said. "I'll take six of these."

"Yes, ma'am," Sue said, mentally adding up the commission and how much closer it would get her to a minivan.

Miz Phelps went back into the dressing room to get

changed, and Ida nodded approvingly at Sue. Then she had to go and ruin it by saying, "Don't forget to wrap them."

"Yes, ma'am." Sue had forgotten once last week, and Ida was never going to let her live it down. She went out back and pulled out five more Model 3000s, making sure to change all of the tags, and then wrapped the bras in the pale pink tissue paper Petticoat Junction stocked.

Wrapping things in paper the customers were going to toss away the second they got home made no sense to Sue, and once again, she wished the store's owner was still running the store. She and Bobbie Jo had gotten along real well, but Bobbie Jo had retired and hired Ida as manager, and suddenly the place had to be highfalutin.

First Ida had moved the store to Rocky Shoals, because she said there was a better class of customer there. Sue didn't mind that because it was closer to her house, but she did mind having to wear dresses and pantyhose to work, and she didn't much care for the other changes Ida had made, either.

Now everything in the store was pink, from the carpet to the curtains to the doors on the dressing rooms. Even the cash register was pink. And now they sold *undergarments* instead of *underwear*, *panties* instead of *drawers*, and *stockings* instead of *pantyhose*. If her station wagon weren't on its last legs, Sue would never have put up with it, and if Bobbie Jo hadn't insisted, Ida never would have kept her. Ida was itching for an excuse to get rid of her because Sue wasn't prissy enough to suit her, but Sue wanted that minivan something fierce. So if Ida wanted her to waste time wrapping bras in tissue paper, Sue would wrap bras in tissue paper.

Sue had to admit that the store was making more money

than when Bobbie Jo was in charge, so maybe Ida knew what she was doing. Who'd have thought women could be so particular about their bras and so embarrassed about what size they wore? Sue herself had no interest in wearing gauzy nothings.

After four breast-fed children, all she wanted was support and comfort, and her own bras made the Le Bustier 3000s look as flimsy as the pink tissue paper they were wrapped in.

Sue was ringing up Miz Phelps' bras when the front door opened, and Ida went to greet the new customers. Sue recognized Tori Dupont, who had been in her graduating class, and Tori's daughter, Marie, who was a friend of Sue's daughter, Tiffany.

"Can I help you ladies?" Ida asked, smiling as warm a smile as she could manufacture.

"I hope so," Tori said while Marie looked in every direction other than at Ida. "My daughter here is ready for her first bra."

Sue would have cussed if she could have. According to Tiffany, Marie was the only girl in her class who didn't wear a bra. Other than Tiffany, that is. Tiffany was as flat as a flounder, but every other day she was whining that she needed a bra and that girls who were flatter than she was wore one. First off, Sue didn't think it was possible to be flatter than Tiffany, and second, if those other girls' mothers wanted to waste money on bras their daughters didn't need, that was their business. The problem was, Tiffany didn't see it that way, and when she saw Marie wearing a bra come Monday morning, she was going to be impossible to live with.

Miz Phelps had paid for her bras and was heading for the door when the mailman came in. Sue couldn't help grinning. As pink as the store was, it was nothing compared to the color that fellow turned every time he had to deliver something. He could get away with sliding letters under the door, but this time he had a package.

"Special delivery," he said in a choked voice.

Sue reached to take it from him, but Ida said, "I'll take care of this, Sue. You help Miz Dupont. And Miss Dupont." She smiled at the girl, but Marie was still trying to find something to look at that wouldn't embarrass her.

Sue took Tori and Marie over to the part of the store that had the sign *New Beginnings* hanging overhead, but Tori and Marie were more interested in seeing what was in that box. People around Rocky Shoals didn't get many special delivery packages. Miz Phelps was waiting around, too. The mailman, on the other hand, left as soon as he got Ida's signature.

"Thank goodness!" Ida said as she ripped the box open, not even bothering to use a letter opener to protect her manicure. She tossed wads of lavender tissue paper out onto the floor before reverently pulling out and unfolding a complete set of salmon pink lingerie: matching bra, panties, camisole, and garter belt. Marie finally stopped looking at her sneakers, and even Sue was impressed.

"That's just what I need for the cotillion," Miz Phelps said, even though it was plain that she'd need two or three sets like that to cover her. "How much is it?"

"I'm sorry, Miz Phelps," Ida said. "This ensemble is already sold. Miz Lamar special ordered it. According to the catalog, these are exactly like what Princess Diana wore on her wedding day. Only hers were white, of course."

The customers oohed and ahhed while Ida pulled out one of the satin padded hangers they used for negligees and delicately arranged the set. Then she hung it on the hook between the two dressing rooms, the place of honor reserved for the store's best. "I was afraid that it wouldn't arrive in time for the cotillion tonight, and Miz Lamar would have been so disappointed."

Disappointed? Sue knew darned well that Miz Lamar would have been mad as a wet hen. No wonder Ida had been a pain all day. Miz Lamar had probably been worrying her to death.

"Sue," Ida said, "clean up this mess while I call Miz Lamar."

Sue tried to smile instead of gritting her teeth as she gathered the box and packing material and took it to the storeroom. When she came back out front, the store's customers were clustered around the royal undergarments.

"Does it come in other colors?" Miz Phelps was asking.

"I believe so," Ida said, "but I have to warn you that it's quite expensive."

Sue whistled softly. It must be high for Ida to admit that to a customer. Ida called a thirty-dollar bra "one of life's necessities," and a forty-dollar bra "a little indulgence."

Ida said, "Come on back to my office to look at the catalog." Sue raised her estimate even more. Ida kept her office fancier than the store itself, and only did business there if she thought she was going to make a big sale.

Sue wasn't pleased. Miz Phelps was her customer, but if Ida made the sale, she wouldn't have to pay Sue a commission. At least she had Tori to wait on. A few bras for Marie should help with the minivan. Sue said, "Marie, put your arms down so I can get a look at you."

Marie wouldn't meet Sue's eyes, but she did move her arms away from her chest, such as it was. She didn't have much more than Tiffany. Sue pulled out three different triple A's, bras so small they had spandex panels instead of cups. "Give these a try, and see which one feels the best. Now remember—you're going to be wearing it all day long. Make sure it's comfortable."

Just then the door opened again, and Lee Fredericks, one of Sue's regular customers, came in. Marie's eyes got wide as saucers because of a man seeing her with bras in her hand, and she fled into the dressing room and slammed the door behind her.

Tori smiled. "I still remember how embarrassed I was when I got my first bra."

Sue didn't see what the big deal was, but she nodded anyway. "If you'll excuse me a minute, I'll go see what Mr. Fredericks needs."

"Hey, Sue," Lee said.

"Hey there, Lee. What can I do you for?"

"I just dropped by to see if you had anything new. For my wife."

"How did she like that last batch of panties?"

"Loved them," he said.

"Well, we've got some new ones in that same line, only the lace is softer. Pretty colors, too."

"Let's see them."

"Did the size tens fit all right?"

"Perfectly," he said, with a gleam in his eye.

Just like with bras, Ida didn't keep the larger sizes on

display, so Sue went out back to get the panties in red, black, dark blue, and pine green. Just for the heck of it, she pulled out some tiger- and leopard-skin prints, too.

She laid them out on a table in front of Lee, and while he looked at them, she went back to the dressing room. "How are you doing in there, Marie?"

"Okay."

"Let me take a look."

Marie only opened the door a crack. She wasn't taking any chances that Lee would be able to see the little bit she had.

Sue peered in. "Turn around."

Marie obeyed.

Sue pulled at the midriff band. "This one's too big. Let me get you a smaller size."

"Smaller than this?" Marie said in anguished tones.

"Not the cup size," Sue explained. "I'm talking about the band. It's got to fit right to support you the way it should."

Sue closed the door so Marie could try on the next one.

Tori whispered, "Did I hear you getting that man size ten panties?"

Sue nodded.

"His wife must be huge! I didn't wear panties that big when I was pregnant with Marie."

Sue shrugged. Lee lived in Charlotte, so she didn't have any idea of what his wife looked like. Besides, the woman never got any of those panties he picked out anyway. Sue had figured out ages ago that he wore them himself, and he probably had a pair on under his khakis right now. Why else would he buy panties in Rocky Shoals, when there were plenty of bigger places in Charlotte? Size ten was big for a woman, but it wasn't big at all for a man.

"Marie," Sue said, "I'm handing you the other size over the door."

Marie's hand reached up to take them.

Tori said, "You know, while I'm here, I may as well get a couple of new bras, too."

Sue looked over at Lee to make sure he was all right, and saw him admiring the salmon pink lingerie set. She was pretty sure that garter belts were too much for him, but she sure would have liked the commission from selling it to him. Anyway, since he was occupied, she helped Tori look for what she wanted. Except they didn't have what she wanted. That model had been discontinued.

"But I've been wearing the same exact bra since high school," Tori said.

"You did develop all at once, didn't you?" Sue said. Tori had left school at the end of freshmen year flat as a pancake, but had had all the boys chasing after her when she came back in September. "Le Bustier makes one that's nearly the same. Try one on and see what you think."

"Are you sure I can't get the old one?"

Sue sighed. Not only were women particular about bras, but some were loyal until death. "You might be able to call around and find somebody who's got one left, but you may as well go ahead and get used to something else." She pulled one from a rack. "Try this one and tell me if you don't like it just as well."

"I don't need to try it on."

"You heard what I told Marie. An uncomfortable bra can ruin your whole day."

Sue handed it to her, and Tori disappeared into the dressing room. While she was gone, Sue spoke to Lee, then went into the back room to get him more of the animal-print panties.

Sue was trying to make sure everybody had everything they needed when Annabelle Lamar swept in, nose as high in the air as ever. Ignoring the fact that Sue was busy with other customers, she said, "I'm here to pick up my order."

Ida must have heard her, because she pushed Miz Phelps out of her office so she could usher Miz Lamar in. Then she rushed back out to get the salmon pink lingerie and say, "Sue, I told you to get that trash off of the floor."

With so many customers in the store, Sue couldn't even cuss under her breath as she grabbed a wad of white tissue she'd missed and shoved it into her pocket. It wasn't as though she didn't have plenty to do. Lee was waiting to pay for his panties, Miz Phelps wanted her to write up the catalog order, Tori had decided to get the new bra but wanted Sue to find her two more, and Marie couldn't make up her mind which bra felt the best.

Sue was trying to get them all squared away when Miz Lamar realized that her panties were missing.

Now Sue was trying her darnedest to figure out what had happened. She hated to admit it, but Miz Lamar was right. Somebody in the store had to have those panties.

Miz Lamar said, "Ida, if you won't call the police, I'll do it myself."

Not that she actually reached for the phone, of course. She was too used to people doing whatever she wanted. So that gave Sue enough time to think the situation over.

The way Sue figured it, if Ida had wanted to take the panties, she wouldn't have made a point of opening the box in front of everybody. Besides which, she'd own up to it now to keep Miz Lamar from calling the police. As for Miz Lamar, Sue wouldn't put it past her because the woman enjoyed making a fuss, but she didn't think she'd had a chance.

That left the other customers. The lingerie had been hanging in plain sight, and since Sue and Ida had been going back and forth to the storeroom and office, there'd been plenty of time for somebody to grab them.

Sue didn't think even Miz Phelps could convince herself that she could stuff herself into those panties—Miz Lamar had to be fifty pounds lighter than Miz Phelps. And Miz Phelps had enough money to buy herself a set of her own if she wanted it. Of course, she and Miz Lamar were both involved in what passed for high society in Rocky Shoals, and Sue knew that fancy cotillions meant fancy feuds. Could Miz Phelps have taken the panties just to get Miz Lamar's goat?

Then there was Lee Fredericks. But wearing women's panties was one thing, stealing them was another. Not to mention the fact that he couldn't wear them any more than Miz Phelps could. Besides, Lee had the most to lose by being caught—a story like that could easily reach all the way to Charlotte, especially if he was found wearing the baby blue panties he'd bought last time. Sue really didn't want it to be him anyway. Commissions from his shopping trips had already paid for the spare tire on the minivan, and she was hoping for a stereo.

That left Marie and Tori. As embarrassed as Marie

was about bras, would she have risked being caught stealing panties? Especially panties that were way too big for her. Tori could have worn them, but if she was the kind to always buy the same bra, Sue didn't think she was likely to have a sudden urge to wear fancy panties.

So nobody needed or wanted the panties, and Sue couldn't see somebody stealing them just to torment Miz Lamar. Of course, it was Ida who was in trouble, and Ida made people mad every day, but Sue could think of a whole lot better ways of getting back at her than stealing panties. As for Sue herself, even if she'd annoyed one of the customers that much, there were worse things they could do to her, too.

Sue stuck her hands in her pockets, a habit Ida said wasn't businesslike or ladylike. That's when she figured it out. "Hold on a minute. Maybe those panties are still in the box. I better go check." Ida started to protest, but Sue talked over her. "Just so it doesn't look like I'm pulling something, I'm going to take somebody in the back with me to look. Tori, how about you?"

Tori looked reluctant, so Sue added, "Marie will be all right for a minute."

Tori nodded and followed her into the storeroom.

Once they were out of earshot, Sue took a good look at Tori and deliberately poked her friend on the right side of her chest. It made a noise, like crinkling paper. Then Sue poked the left side. There was no noise, but she knew doggoned well that she wasn't poking the woman's boob either.

"Tori, how long have you been stuffing your bra?"

Tori's face turned bright red, but she knew she'd been caught. "Ever since high school."

"Why would you do such a fool thing?"

"Because I was the last one in our class to need a bra. Don't you remember?"

"What about Lou Ann?"

"I saw her the summer after freshman year, and she'd started wearing one, so I got one of my own and— And I stuffed it."

"Geez, Tori."

"You don't know how it felt, Sue. You got your bosom in junior high school. Nobody ever laughed at you."

"Nobody ever laughed at me because I wouldn't let them," Sue pointed out.

"I guess you're right," Tori said, "but I was pretty insecure back then."

If she was still stuffing her bra, Sue figured that she must still be mighty insecure. "You do have a bosom now, don't you?"

"Of course I do, but it's not as big as I'd made myself out to be. I knew people would notice if I changed sizes, so as I got bigger, I used less and less stuffing. I thought sure I'd catch up some day, but I never did."

Did Tori really think people paid that much attention the size of her boobs? What did she do about her husband? Sue shook her head, just not understanding. Then she reached into her pocket and pulled out the wad of tissue paper that Ida had told her to pick up. "Is this yours?"

"Is that what happened to it? It rolled out of the dressing room while I was trying on the new bra, and I couldn't find it. I had to find something to put in my bra—otherwise it would have showed!"

She was right. The shirt she was wearing would have

made it pretty obvious. It was too tight for her to hide any-thing. Other than Miz Lamar's panties, that is.

Tori went on. "I looked out of the dressing room, but the only thing within reach was Miz Lamar's lingerie. I was meaning to come out of the dressing room and find some-thing else to use, and then put the panties back. I didn't mean to cause any trouble."

"There's not going to be any trouble." Sue held out her hand. "Give 'em here."

Tori reached into her bra and pulled out the crumpled panties. Sue gave her the stuffing back, then took the panties and shoved them into a corner of the shipping box. "Just agree with whatever I say, all right?" They went back into the store, with Sue carrying the box.

"Are they in there?" Ida asked, the strain showing in her voice.

"I'm not sure." Sue made a big show of pulling out tissue paper, then acted real surprised when she found the panties. "Well, here they are. They must have been here all along."

Miz Lamar looked suspicious, but Sue and Tori looked innocent, so there was nothing she could say other than to demand a discount for them being so wrinkled. Ida took care of it while Sue handled the other customers.

Miz Phelps still looked indignant, and Sue was willing to bet there were going to be fireworks at the cotillion. Marie and Tori just acted glad to be getting out of there, but Tori did turn back and mouth, "Thank you," to Sue. Lee had one eyebrow raised as if he thought Sue had pulled something, but was too nice to say so. He did loudly mention that Sue ought to get a bonus for saving them all a lot of trouble. When Miz Lamar agreed, Ida gritted her teeth and said they were right.

By the time they were all gone, there was only an hour or so until closing time, and Sue spent most of that hour looking at the *New Beginnings* bras. Come closing time, Sue wrapped up five of the smallest, daintiest bras Petticoat Junction sold. She figured that with her employee discount, she was still making a profit from the bonus Ida had promised her. Maybe Tiffany didn't have anything to fill the bras with, but Sue would rather she wear them empty now as to go on a panty raid twelve years down the road.

Bible Belt

This story takes place in Rocky Shoals, the town adjacent to Byerly. Belva also appears in Tight as a Tick, *and both Belva and Wynette appear in* Wed and Buried. *(Belva appears in another story in this collection, too.)*

It took Wynette a while to find the Ten Commandments in the Bible Reverend Sweeney had left for her to read while she was in the hospital. She thought they'd be marked, but they were just stuck in with the other verses. Finally she found them in the book of Exodus. There were command-ments about stealing and killing and coveting, but nothing against hitting your wife.

There was nothing about doing other things to your wife, either. Wynette found the commandment about adultery, but that was just for people who weren't married. With Duke being her husband, it must be okay with God for him to throw her onto the bed and do whatever he wanted. If it wasn't, He'd have made a commandment against it.

The next chapter had all kinds of other rules, and she read them, too. They weren't commandments, exactly, but since they were in the Bible, they must be God's will. There was a lot about smiting men and neighbors, mothers and fathers, and even servants, but nothing about smiting wives. She'd have thought that a wife was more important than a servant, but maybe God didn't see it that way.

Then Wynette found something about how you shouldn't make a woman miscarry, but when she read the rest of the verse, she saw it only counted if it was another man's wife. Did that mean that God didn't mind that Duke had made her miscarry his own child?

Could it fit under killing? Reverend Sweeney said abortion was murder, that just because a baby wasn't born yet didn't mean he wasn't a baby. Or she. Dr. Patel hadn't told her which hers was—it was probably too little for him to tell. Anyway, Wynette knew from her cousin that an abortion didn't hurt nearly as much as Duke hitting her in the stomach had.

Duke had told Dr. Patel he hadn't known she was pregnant, even though he had, so wasn't that bearing false witness? But the Bible only said you couldn't bear false witness against your neighbor, nothing about bearing false witness against your wife. Of course, Wynette had gone to Sunday school enough to know that *neighbor* in the Bible wasn't the same as a neighbor who lived next to you. "Love thy neighbor" was supposed to apply to everybody, but maybe God didn't care what men did to their wives. It seemed to Wynette that if He did, He'd have done something about Duke a long time ago. If not the first time he slapped her, then later on, when it got bad. Why hadn't God done something when Duke hit her so hard she lost a tooth? Or the time he cracked her ribs?

She tried to read more, but the talk about oxen and feasts confused her. The print was awfully small, and her head was spinning from the medicine they'd given her. Besides, it didn't look as if God had anything to say about her. That seemed funny, because she'd gone to church every week until she got married. Then she had to quit, because Duke went out on Saturday nights and it bothered him for her to take a shower and get dressed the next morning. Now when she woke up on Sundays, she'd lie in the bed waiting for him to stir before she got up. Sometimes she had to pee so bad it hurt, but she could stand that a whole lot easier than she could stand what a hungover Duke would do if he were woken early.

Wynette carefully closed the Bible and put it on the nightstand next to the bed. She wasn't sure if Reverend Sweeney had been giving it to her or only loaning it, so she wanted to be sure to take care of it. Then she looked for the TV control, but it was out of her reach. She didn't think Duke had put it there on purpose, because it would have been easier for him to not rent the TV for her in the first place. Besides, he was always nice to her when she was in the hospital.

She thought about calling a nurse to get her the control, but the nurses must have more important things to worry about than her. The hospital was filled with sick people, and Wynette wasn't really sick. The doctor had said she'd be able to try and have another baby. Only next time she'd make sure Duke was ready to start a family.

Wynette had expected her husband to be as excited as she was about the news. She'd been in the bedroom putting on makeup when Duke got home from work, because it was

Friday night and she'd thought sure he'd want to go out to celebrate. But before she could tell him, he started in on her because she'd forgotten to get more beer. He'd hit her once or maybe twice before she could say anything, and then she'd blurted it out, not at all the way she'd planned, just to make him stop. Only it didn't make him stop. Hearing about the baby just made him madder. By the time Duke had stopped hurting her, their baby was dead.

Now Wynette knew that she was going to have to make sure she didn't get pregnant again until Duke said it was okay. The thing was, he wouldn't use a rubber. Birth control pills cost money, and Duke wasn't the type to pay attention to a calendar when he was in the mood. Maybe she could get a diaphragm. Her sister, Lynn, didn't use hers anymore, so Wynette could borrow it and it wouldn't cost Duke anything.

There was a tap at the door, and Wynette looked up and saw Belva Tucker.

"Hey, Wynette," Belva said.

"Hey, Belva."

Belva came in, and pulled one of the chairs over close to the bed so they could talk without Wynette having to hold her head up. Belva was always thoughtful that way. Some people thought Belva wasn't gentle the way a woman should be because of her being one of Rocky Shoals' deputies, but Wynette knew better. She always came to see Wynette when she was in the hospital or sick. Most times she brought candy or a magazine or even flowers.

Belva must have remembered that, too, because she said, "I'm embarrassed I don't have anything for you. I came to see Dr. Patel, and I didn't even know you were here until he mentioned it." She hesitated a minute. "I'm awfully sorry about the baby."

"That's all right, Belva. It's probably for the best."

"You mean because of Duke?" Belva asked, and Wynette could tell that her friend was mad.

"Of course not," Wynette said quickly, not wanting Belva mad at her. "I just mean that there must have been something wrong with the baby or God wouldn't have taken him. Reverend Sweeney said God was being merciful."

Belva didn't look as if she believed Wynette or Reverend Sweeney, but she nodded anyway. "Is there anything I can get you?"

"You don't have to bring me anything, Belva. They're taking good care of me."

"They ought to. They see you enough." Before Wynette had a chance to answer that, Belva added, "I bet you wouldn't turn down a bag of Hershey's Kisses."

Wynette grinned and managed to keep from wincing, even though her mouth still hurt from where Duke had slapped her. "Belva, have you ever known me to turn down Hershey's Kisses?"

"Then I'll be sure and bring you some tomorrow after church."

"Aren't you sweet. But I might not be here that long. Dr. Patel says I might can go home in the morning."

"That's all right——I'll find you," she said with a grin. But she got that mad look again before she said, "Are you going to be needing a place to stay when you get out of here?"

Wynette tried to pretend she didn't know what Belva meant. "Of course not. Duke will be here to take me home."

Belva nodded and sighed a little, as if she was sad about something.

Just to get her thinking about something else, Wynette said, "Are you still chasing after those hijackers?"

"You know me——I never give up," Belva said, and from the tone of her voice, Wynette knew she wasn't just talking about hijackers. "That's why I'm up here, as a matter of fact. They found another trucker with his head bashed in this morning."

"Is he going to be all right?"

"He should recover, but it's going to be a few days before I can talk to him. There's no telling where those bastards will be by then." She politely added, "Pardon my French."

"That's all right," Wynette said. Lord knows Duke said worse than that every day, and besides, she didn't blame Belva for cussing. For months, a band of hijackers had been tormenting truckers all up and down the highways of North Carolina, and they seemed to be centered around their area. According to the TV news, the whole state depended on the trucking industry, which Wynette hadn't realized before. So if truckers started getting scared and taking jobs elsewhere, it could hurt everybody. And the truckers had every right to be scared—one man had already been killed.

"You'd think the truckers would stop picking up hitchhikers," Wynette said.

Belva said, "This one didn't. They found him at a rest stop, and it looks as if that's where he was attacked. I'm guessing he stopped to take a leak, and they jumped him in the john. From now on, I bet the truckers are going to be peeing in empty bottles rather than stop anywhere around here."

"What was he carrying? Was it valuable?"

"We're still trying to find out. The hijackers took all the paperwork along with the truck. It looks as if they're just hitting trucks at random, anyway. They sell the loads for whatever they can get, strip the trucks of anything else worth selling, and dump the rest." She looked at her watch. "Well, I better be getting on. You call if you need anything."

"Thanks, but Duke will be here later."

Belva made a noise that was almost a snort as she got up from her chair. She was halfway out the door when she turned back and asked, "Come to think of it, where was your husband last night?"

"Duke? He was here with me." Once he realized how badly hurt she was, he'd driven her right to the hospital.

"All night?"

"Well, he went home at bedtime, of course." Wynette had hoped he'd come back that morning, since it was Saturday and he didn't have to work, but with Reverend Sweeney and Belva visiting, she hadn't been too lonely. "Why do you ask?"

"Just wondering."

"Belva, you've been working too hard," Wynette said, trying to make it sound as if it were a joke. "You'll be seeing hijackers under the bed before long." She smiled as if she knew Belva was kidding.

Belva didn't smile back——she just looked at her as if there were something she wanted to say. Then she put the TV control right where Wynette could reach it before she left.

Wynette kept smiling until Belva was gone, even though it hurt her lip. Once, a long time ago, Wynette had called

Belva after Duke beat her up. Belva had arrested Duke, even put handcuffs on him, but Wynette just couldn't let her take him away. She had still loved him then, so she swore to Belva that it was the first time it had happened, and that she was sure it wouldn't happen again.

That night was the last time she could remember going to church, other than weddings and funerals. She'd asked Reverend Sweeney to unlock the door for her, and she stayed there for hours asking forgiveness for lying to Belva about it being the first time, and then begging God to make the second part come true, to make sure Duke never hit her again. She didn't want Him to strike Duke down with lightning or anything——she just wanted him to quit hitting her. Was that too much of a miracle to ask for? Maybe it was, because God didn't listen. So that meant she'd lied to Belva twice, and she still felt bad about it. Three times, now, she realized. Duke had left way before bedtime the night before.

Wynette turned on the TV, but there was nothing on but ball games, so she turned the sound way down, but didn't shut off the set because Duke was paying good money for her to have that TV in her room.

Wynette looked over at the Bible. Reverend Sweeney had said that God did everything for a reason, which meant that He must have a reason for letting Duke hit her. Was it something she'd done? Whatever it was, it must have been something awfully bad. She was trying to think of what it could be when she fell asleep.

The next thing she knew, the evening news was on and Duke had the control and was turning the sound up so he could hear it.

"Hey, Duke," she said, croaking a little because her throat was dry.

He poured some water into a plastic cup, and held it for her to drink, even though she could have done it herself.

"The ice melted," he said. "I'll tell the nurse to get you some fresh."

She smiled at him. "That's all right. This is plenty cold."

He helped her take another sip, then started to put the water pitcher down on top of the Bible on the nightstand.

"Don't put it there," Wynette said. Then she saw the look in his eye. "I mean, let me get this out of your way." She reached for the Bible, meaning to put it into the drawer of the nightstand, but Duke took it from her first.

"Where'd that come from?" he asked.

"Reverend Sweeney came to visit this morning and left it for me."

"Why? Does he think we can't afford a Bible?"

"Of course not," Wynette said quickly. "He was just being nice."

"Next time you see him, you tell him that when you need a Bible, I'll get you one."

"I'll be sure to. I was going to give him that one back anyway."

Duke nodded, but he put the Bible back on the nightstand and made a point of putting the pitcher right on top of it. "Are they treating you all right? You tell me if they don't."

"They're being real nice."

"They damn well better be. I'm paying them enough."

No matter what happened in private, Duke made sure everybody else treated her the way they should.

"I've been talking to the doctor," he said, looking serious. "We think it would be better if you went ahead and had a— If they gave you a—"

"What, Duke? Is there something else wrong?" She breathed in sharply. "It's not cancer, is it?" Her mama had died from cancer, and her daddy's father had been sick with cancer when he had his heart attack. That meant she had it on both sides.

"No, it's nothing like that."

"It's not—" She couldn't even say AIDS out loud. She'd never slept with anybody but Duke, but she knew Duke had been with other women before they got married, and probably since then, too.

"You're not sick," Duke said, with that edge in his voice that told her she better not interrupt him again. "It's just that we think you ought to get your tubes tied so you don't get pregnant again, not after what happened this time."

"But Dr. Patel said I could get pregnant again in a few months."

"It's not getting pregnant that's the problem. He says you can't carry a child."

"Why not? Why didn't he tell me?"

Duke shrugged. "I guess he didn't know for sure right off. But he looked at your test results and figured it out after I told him about your family history, the way your sister and your mama lost all those babies."

"Lots of women lose babies," Wynette protested. "I heard on *Oprah* that half the women in America miscarry. Almost all of them go on to have babies."

"Maybe so, but you can't. There's something wrong with

you, otherwise you wouldn't have lost this one just from falling down a couple of steps."

That's what Duke had told Dr. Patel, that she'd fallen. She'd been surprised that he believed it, but Dr. Patel was young and new in town. Besides, Duke had a way of saying things that kept most folks from arguing with him.

He went on. "Anyway, he said we ought to take care of it while you're still here in the hospital. We've already met the deductible, so it won't cost us a penny more than what we owe now."

No more pennies, Wynette thought, but it'd cost her all her babies. "Is he sure?" she asked anxiously. "Can't he do some more tests? Or get a second opinion. Oprah says that you should never have something serious done without getting a second opinion."

"It'd just be a waste of money," Duke said. "You can't carry a child and I'm not about to keep carting you up here to the hospital every time you get yourself knocked up."

"But Duke—"

"Besides, I don't want any children."

"Duke!" she said in a shocked whisper. "You never told me that. When we got married, you said you wanted a house full of kids."

"That was before I saw how much trouble they are. Look at your sister's crew. A man can't hardly hear himself think with those three rug-rats running around. They're loud, and they talk back, and they make the worst mess I've ever seen."

"I can keep kids quiet, Duke—they don't talk back if they're taught not to. And I can keep the house clean. Don't I get it all cleaned up when you have your poker games, even before you get up the next morning?"

There was a glint in Duke's eye, as if he thought she was criticizing him, but he let it go and Wynette relaxed. Then he said, "You can't carry a child anyway, so none of that makes any difference. They've scheduled the surgery for first thing Monday morning. It'll be over with before you know it, and if everything goes the way it's supposed to, you'll be home Tuesday."

"Do we have to do it so soon?"

"It's already been scheduled," he said impatiently. He picked up a clipboard with a bunch of papers that had been lying at the foot of the bed. "You need to sign these."

"What are they?" she said, taking them from him and starting to read the one on top.

"Just sign where I tell you," he said, sticking a ballpoint pen into her hand.

"Oprah says that you should never sign anything without reading it first."

"I don't care *what* that black bitch says," he said quietly, so nobody passing by could hear. "Just sign it!"

Wynette thought about her sister's children, the two girls and a boy Lynn had carried with no trouble at all, even if she had lost her first baby. And she thought about the trash bag filled with hand-me-down baby clothes that Lynn had given her. It didn't seem right that those clothes would never get worn again. Didn't the Bible say that wasting was a sin?

Then she pictured a little girl limping when she walked, the way Wynette did that time Duke kicked her so hard. She imagined a boy with her daddy's blue eyes, but not hardly being able to tell what color they were because of swelling. Surely God didn't want that to happen. So maybe

He didn't want her to have babies. Maybe it was like Reverend Sweeney had said, that this was God's way of being merciful.

She signed the papers.

Duke said, "I've got to give these to the nurse, and then I'm heading out."

"So soon? The nurse said husbands can stay as late as they want to."

"I've already wasted most of the weekend here, and I've got things to do. I have to call old man Crawford to see about getting a substitute for Monday morning, and then I need to get me something to eat. You never did the grocery shopping."

"Will you be back tomorrow?"

"I don't know. It depends."

Wynette wondered if Duke meant to go out drinking with the boys or maybe even with one of the other women she'd always suspected. "But you will be here Monday morning for the operation, won't you?"

"Why the hell would I need a substitute if I wasn't going to be here?"

"I'm so glad," she said, smiling at him.

Only he didn't see it because he was reaching for his ball cap, and muttering, "Maybe Crawford will let me make the time up so I don't have to use any of my vacation time."

"Good night, Duke." But he was already gone.

After the nurse brought her dinner, Wynette watched TV for a little while, but she had to change channels whenever anything with children came on the screen. Then she tried to call her sister, but when there was no answer, she remembered that Lynn and her family had gone to Myrtle

Beach for the weekend. Wynette had written the name of the hotel where they were staying on the pad beside the phone at home, but she couldn't remember it and knew that calling Duke would be a waste of time. Even if he was home, he probably wouldn't want her calling Lynn. Maybe it was just as well. By the time Lynn got back Sunday night, visiting hours would be over anyway. She'd have to wait to talk to her after the... Afterward.

Wynette closed her eyes, but she couldn't sleep. She just kept thinking of the way babies smell and the little noises they make. Duke was right about Lynn's children being wild, but her sister wasn't good with children the way Wynette was. It was Wynette who'd babysat the kids at church during services, and watched over the younger cousins at family weddings and such. Lynn had said herself that the only reason her three minded as well as they did was because of the time Wynette had spent with them before she and Duke got married.

She wriggled in the bed, trying to get comfortable. Maybe Duke would let her spend more time over at Lynn's after she got back home. That would be almost as good as having her own kids, wouldn't it? She rolled over and saw the Bible still sitting on the nightstand. The pitcher of water on top of it had sweated so that there was a ring of water on the black leatherette cover, hiding the words *Holy Bible*.

Wynette's mama had always told her to never put anything on top of a Bible, not even another book, so she knew she should move the pitcher and wipe off the water before it ruined the cover. She didn't—she just looked at it, watching more droplets form and run down the sides of the pitcher and onto the Bible. She wondered if Reverend Sweeney would be mad at her, or if God Himself would be mad at her. Then she snorted. What had God ever done for her? He'd given her Duke and taken away her babies. Mad at her? Well, damn it, she was mad at Him, too!

"Damn it," she said, but in a whisper, as if lightning would strike if she said it too loud. Nothing happened, not even when she repeated it a minute later. It seemed pretty plain that God wasn't listening to her. Maybe He never had.

She said, "Damn it," once more, this time in a good, strong voice. Then she rolled over and went to sleep, leaving the pitcher to drip onto the Bible.

The next morning, the nurses helped Wynette get up and walk around, and it didn't hurt nearly as bad as she thought it would. It seemed as if it should hurt more to lose a baby. Of course, she'd heard that having tubes tied didn't hurt much at all, and having that done would lose Wynette her babies for good.

Then the nurse asked if she wanted help going down to the chapel on the first floor for what she called non-denominational services. Wynette started to say that she did, but then she remembered that she didn't care about what God wanted anymore. So she said she didn't feel up to it.

The only thing was, that didn't leave her anything to do with herself. Somebody would come in once in a while to check on her, and people came by to deliver meal trays and clean the bathroom, but otherwise, she was left alone. Reverend Sweeney's Bible was still on the nightstand, but Wynette didn't even look at it. Instead she watched TV and dozed all day long.

The door to her room opening woke her late in the afternoon, and she put on a welcoming smile for her husband, but it was Belva who walked into the room.

"Hey there, Belva," she said, not having to fake the smile anymore.

"Hey there, yourself. I brought you something." She held out a tin that was decorated to look like a merry-go-round.

"Isn't that the cutest thing!" Wynette said, delighted.

"No big deal," Belva said. "I was just going to get a bag of kisses, but every time I open one of those bags, I spill the candy all over everywhere, so I thought you might want something to keep them in."

"Thank you, Belva."

"I was afraid I'd missed you. I meant to get by sooner, but I had to go into work after church."

"Actually, I'm going to be here for a couple more days," Wynette said, trying to sound casual about it.

Belva's eyes narrowed. "Did Duke—"

Wynette quickly said, "It's because I'm having surgery tomorrow morning."

"Is something wrong?"

"No, I'm just getting my tubes tied."

"I thought you wanted children."

Wynette looked away, not wanting to talk about her failings. It was embarrassing enough that Duke and Dr. Patel knew there was something wrong with her. "I guess I changed my mind."

That's when Duke walked in. "What's she doing here?" he said to Wynette, glaring at the deputy.

"I'm visiting Wynette," Belva said. "Is that a problem, Cloyd?"

They always talked that way. Duke called Belva *Deputy*

Tucker because he didn't think a woman should be a police officer, and Belva called him *Cloyd* because she knew that he hated his given name.

"I hear there aren't going to be any little Cloyds," Belva said. "I suppose we should thank the Lord for small favors."

Duke's face changed colors the way it did when he got mad but couldn't do anything about it. "I'd just as soon you didn't make fun of my wife. It's not her fault that her parts aren't right."

Belva turned to Wynette. "Is that true?"

Wynette nodded.

In a much softer voice, Belva said, "I'm sorry, Wynette. Why didn't you say something?"

Wynette shrugged, her throat too tight to talk.

"You're sure there's nothing they can do about it?"

Duke said, "I think the doctor can do his job without your help, Deputy. In fact, I think the whole town would be a lot better off without you sticking your nose into everybody's business."

Belva stepped forward until she was right in Duke's face, and just stared at him while his face got redder. Cloyd leaned closer to her, as if he wanted her to move out of his way, but Belva didn't so much as move a muscle. Wynette could tell from the way her husband was breathing that he wanted to hit Belva something fierce, but he didn't dare, not with her being a deputy. Finally he had to back down, and aimed his glare at Wynette instead.

"What's that?" he asked, thumping the can on her lap.

"Just some candy Belva brought me," Wynette said. "Do you want some?"

"Hell, no," he snapped, picking the can up and putting

it on the nightstand, on top of the Bible. "You shouldn't be eating candy anyway."

"The nurses said—" Wynette saw his face darken and said, "You're probably right, Duke. I don't suppose it's good for me."

"I brought you something *nice*," he said, looking at Belva pointedly as he dropped a heavy book on Wynette's lap.

"It's a Bible," Wynette said, surprised. Covered in white imitation leather, it had a color picture of Jesus on the cover, and gold curlicues and plastic gemstones framing the picture. She'd never seen a such a flashy Bible.

"You can tell Reverend Sweeney that he can just take that cheap copy back," Duke said.

Now Wynette understood. Reverend Sweeney hadn't meant anything by leaving her the Bible, but Duke couldn't stand the idea that somebody might think he couldn't afford one for her. Or maybe he didn't even want her talking to God without knowing what was being said. Still, it was a nice gift, and she said, "Thank you, Duke. This sure is something."

"Yeah, it sure is," Belva said. "You must have had to go all the way to Charlotte to find something that fancy." Only she didn't sound as if she thought "fancy" was a good thing, and Duke clenched his jaw.

"You didn't go to all that trouble, did you, Duke?" Wynette asked, worried that he'd hold it over her if he had.

"Of course not," Duke snapped. "I bought it at the flea market, not that it's any of Deputy Tucker's business."

"A flea market Bible," Belva said. "Why am I not surprised?"

Duke shot Belva a dirty look, but with no way to get the

mad out of his system, he reached into his back pocket for his pack of Winstons.

"You can't smoke in here," Belva said with a mean smile. "It's against the law, which means that I'd have to arrest you if you lit up."

"There's laws about police harassment, too, you know," Duke said, shoving the cigarettes back into his pocket, and he stomped out of the room.

"Wynette, are you sure you want to go through with this?" Belva said as soon as he was gone. "You don't have to make up your mind right now. You just had a miscarriage—don't you want to take a few days to think it over?"

"It's all been arranged, Belva."

"Have you talked to your sister? What does she think?"

"I couldn't get her. Besides, it wouldn't make any difference."

"What about Reverend Sweeney? Did you speak to him?"

"I don't think he can help me, Belva. Not with this." She couldn't imagine talking to any man about not being able to carry a baby.

"Listen to me," Belva said, touching Wynette's hand. "You don't have to put up with what Duke does to you. There's services and shelters and people who understand what you're going through. There's places you can get help."

Wynette wanted to believe her, she really did, but she just didn't. She looked down in her lap, and opened the Bible to the front, where they'd put in spaces to record family births. Almost without her realizing it, tears started to roll onto her face and onto the page.

"Oh, Wynette," Belva said, closing the Bible and taking it away. "Why won't you let me help you?"

"Nobody can help me, Belva." From over her friend's shoulder, she saw Duke come back into the room. "You better go."

Belva took a deep breath, and let it out slowly. "All right. I'll be back tomorrow to check on you."

Duke said, "That won't be necessary, Deputy. I've told the nurses that I don't want you bothering my wife anymore."

Belva didn't so much as look at him. "I'll see you tomorrow, Wynette." Then she did something kind of peculiar. She started to put Wynette's new Bible on the nightstand, but stopped and looked at the back cover. Then she looked up at Duke with her eyes narrowed before heading for the door.

"Bitch!" Duke said, long before Belva was out of earshot. "She's got no business coming here."

"I like Belva," Wynette said, not willing to let him bad-mouth her friend. "She's always real nice to me."

"Of course she's nice. She's trying to get into your pants."

"Duke!"

"Hell, Wynette, anybody with two eyes can see that she's nothing but a bull dyke. Why do you think I keep telling her to stay away from you?"

Wynette didn't believe it, but she knew better than to argue with Duke.

He stayed around a little while longer, but Wynette suspected it was mostly to make sure Belva didn't come back. She tried to make conversation with him about what else he'd seen at the flea market, but all he wanted to do was watch TV. When the nurse brought in Wynette's dinner tray, he told her he'd see her in the morning, took a handful of candy from her merry-go-round can, and left.

Wynette wasn't all that hungry, but she dutifully ate her food, and when the nurse offered her something to help her sleep, she took that, too. The last thing she wanted was to be up all night thinking.

Two nurses woke her up early the next morning, even earlier than she usually got up to fix Duke's breakfast. They put an IV in her arm and did things to get her ready for the operation. Then they left her alone for a long time, and she wondered why they hadn't just let her sleep the extra half an hour, so she wouldn't worry so much. She knew from *Oprah* that having tubes tied was a routine procedure, but she was feeling awfully nervous by the time Duke finally showed up, a little while after the time the operation was scheduled for.

"Haven't they started yet?" he demanded.

"Not yet. I was afraid you wouldn't make it in time." It was hard to keep that last part from sounding critical, but Wynette couldn't help it. It seemed to her that the least Duke could do was to be there for her surgery.

He shot her a look, but must not have been sure how she meant it. "I got caught in the traffic on Highway 321——I bet the doctor got stuck in it, too. Haven't you heard what's going on out there?"

She shook her head.

"Those morons we've got for police around here finally caught up with the hijackers! Then the hijackers tried to make a break for it, and took off down the highway in a stolen tractor-trailer, but they jackknifed and spilled the load all over the highway. You never saw such a commotion in your life. Must have been a dozen police cruisers there, and reporters, and a clean-up crew, and I don't know who all was wandering around, getting in the way."

Duke turned on the TV, looking for more news about the wreck. After watching the live coverage, Wynette didn't blame Duke for being late. Traffic was still backed up for miles.

Eventually the nurse came in and told them the doctor had finally arrived, and that they'd be ready in a little while. Duke went to get a cup of coffee, but said he'd be back before they took her into the operating room.

Just to distract herself, Wynette kept watching the news, even though they kept repeating the same story over and over again. They said part of the problem with the traffic was the boxes of cargo all over the highway, and the way cars were going out of their way to keep from hitting them.

"I wonder what's in those boxes," Wynette said to herself.

"Bibles," a voice said. Belva was standing at the door. "They've got most of them out of the way, but people won't drive fast because they're afraid of running over a Bible. Don't that beat all?"

"Bibles?" Wynette said.

"That's right. You know how they call this part of the country the Bible Belt? One of the reporters from Charlotte said he's going to start calling 321 the Bible Beltway." Her friend shook her head. "I never saw so many big white Bibles with pictures of Jesus on the cover."

"Is that right?" Wynette said feebly, trying not to look over at the one Duke had brought her the day before.

Duke came in then, and when he say Belva, he thundered, "I told them to keep you out of here!"

Belva just grinned. "Sorry about that, Cloyd. I just came by to tell Wynette about catching the hijackers. I thought she'd want to know, what with you being involved and all."

Wynette swallowed hard, thinking of all the nights Duke had been gone with no explanation. "Belva, you're not saying that Duke...?" She couldn't find the right words to finish the question.

"Him?" Belva said with a sneer. "Cloyd a hijacker? Not hardly. Cloyd isn't even in their league. The hijackers are career criminals, not pissants who beat up on women."

"Why you—!" Duke started, his face nearly purple with rage.

Belva went on as if he hadn't spoken. "No, what led us to the hijackers was that Bible Cloyd bought for you at the flea market. All he cared about was getting one cheap, so he didn't notice what was written on the back. It's printed right on there that this is a special gift for members of the PTL Club in Charlotte. A lot of those televangelists send prizes to people who send in enough money, but they don't actually sell them, so they shouldn't have had any at the flea market. That got me to thinking about that last truck that got hijacked. The driver was still unconscious, so he couldn't tell us what he'd been carrying, so I called the PTL Club, and sure enough, they were expecting a delivery. The flea market had already closed when I found out, so it took me until this morning to track down the folks that had been selling the Bibles. When I found them, darned if they didn't have the stolen truck. I called for backup, they ran, and we chased them down. And it was all because of your husband buying a Bible he should have known was stolen."

"Don't blame me if you can't catch a bunch of thieving sons of bitches," Duke said.

Belva smiled, but Wynette thought it looked more like she was baring her teeth. "Maybe they are thieving sons of bitches, but I bet none of them are the kind of weasel who'd lie to his wife about her needing to have her tubes tied."

"What?" Wynette said, not sure she'd heard her friend right.

"Shut your mouth!" Duke bellowed. Wynette didn't know which of them he was talking to, but it didn't matter, because neither of them were listening.

"I suppose you know Dr. Patel got caught in the traffic jam, too," Belva said. "He left his car to come see if we needed his help, and since one of the hijackers had banged his head up pretty good when the truck went over, Patel helped sew him up and then rode over here in the ambulance with him. I came, too, to guard the hijacker, and we got to talking on the way. I knew he was supposed to do your surgery, and apologized for making him late, and he said it was no big deal because it's elective anyway." She repeated the word. "Elective."

"Elective means I don't *have* to have it done," Wynette said slowly.

"That's right. So I asked the doctor why you were doing it, and he told me what Duke said to him. Duke lied, Wynette, high, wide, and handsome."

"What?" Wynette looked over at her husband. He looked as if he were about ready to explode.

Belva said, "He told the doctor there was a history of miscarriages in your family."

"My mama and sister did miscarry."

"He also told Patel that you were an only child because your mother miscarried a dozen times before dying in childbirth."

"That's not true. I've got a sister and two brothers, and Mama only died a few years ago."

"Dr. Patel told Duke that even with what happened with your mother, there's no reason you should have any problems, but Duke told him you don't want to risk it, that you don't want children. That's the only reason he agreed to do the operation."

"Those papers I signed..." Wynette said slowly.

"Those papers said you knew it was an elective procedure."

Wynette put her hands over her face, wanting to hide from it all. But she knew she couldn't hide anymore. "Is it true, Duke? Is it true that there's nothing wrong with me?"

"Who are you going to believe? This bitch or me?"

"You told me I couldn't have babies, when the only reason I can't is because *you* don't want any." She stared at him——he'd done so much to her, but this was unthinkable. "You don't want me to have *anybody*, do you?"

"You listen here," he said, "I'm not going to have any brats squalling all night long, and I'm not going to have dirty diapers stinking up the place, and I'm not going to have my house looking like a pigsty. You're going to have that operation, and that's that."

"Good Lord, Duke," Wynette said. She was trying to take it in, but all she could do was wonder if that counted

as taking the Lord's name in vain. Then she thought about
the hijackers, who'd stolen Bibles, and the Bible Duke had
bought from them, that had helped Belva track them down.
The Bibles blocking the highway had made Dr. Patel late,
which had given Belva a chance to find out that Duke was
lying.

Maybe it wasn't a lightning bolt or parting the Red Sea,
but surely that was some kind of a miracle.

"I'm not having my tubes tied," Wynette said.

"The hell you say!" Duke said.

"You heard me. I'm *not* having my tubes tied." She sat
up as far as she could. "Duke, I've put up with more from
you than any woman should have to, but I'm not putting up
with this. I want babies." Duke started to speak, but before
he could get the words out, she said, "I don't care if you
want any or not, because I'm leaving you anyway."

"Like hell you are!" He raised one hand, but suddenly
Belva was between him and Wynette's bed, her hand on the
butt of her gun.

"You touch her, and I'll take you down right here and
now."

He wanted to push past her, Wynette knew he did, but
for once, *he* was afraid.

"Belva, you know the law better than I do," Wynette
said. "Will I have any trouble getting a divorce?"

"Not hardly," Belva said. "With the hospital records and
the reports I've filed about Cloyd, you could get every dol-
lar he has while you're at it. Hell, with the right judge, you
could get away with killing him." Belva looked as if she
thought that wouldn't be a bad idea.

Wynette watched Duke's face change colors for a few

seconds, then said, "Go away, Duke. I don't want to see you again unless it's in court."

"Oh, you'll see me again," he said. He glared at her, then stomped out.

Wynette watched until he was gone, then said, "That's that."

"It's a start," Belva said, "but you heard what he said. I just know he's going to try something. Even with the law on your side, it's going to be hard."

"I know. Oprah says that when you finally leave an abuser is the most dangerous time." But maybe because she'd already had one miracle, it didn't seem so much to hope for another. "Belva, can you arrest Duke for making me miscarry?"

"You bet. He'll probably get out on bail, but I ought to be able to hold him long enough to get you settled some-place safe. You'll want to get a restraining order against him, too——I can help with that."

"Thank you, Belva."

"And you know what? If I mention to those hijackers just how I found them, they might take care of Cloyd for you."

It was tempting, but Wynette had to say, "That probably wouldn't be a good thing to do." But she did add, "Though it might not hurt to let Duke *think* you were going to do it."

The two of them laughed, and Wynette couldn't remember when a laugh had felt so good.

The nurse came in then and said, "The doctor's ready."

"Well, I'm not," Wynette said, still laughing. "And I sure would appreciate it if you'd get this needle out of my arm."

It took a while for her and Belva to explain enough to satisfy the nurse, and then Dr. Patel had to come hear it for himself, but eventually everything got sorted out. Well, not everything. It was going to take Belva some time to get the warrants and all ready so she could arrest Duke, and once Dr. Patel knew what had really happened to Wynette, he wanted to run more tests to make sure she was all right. So she was going to have to spend another night in the hospital. But now that she knew it was the last time, she didn't mind so much.

Once she was alone, Wynette reached for her Bible. She'd given the stolen one to Belva for evidence, but she still had the one Reverend Sweeney had given her. She looked at the cover closely, but it didn't look as if the dripping water pitcher had left a mark after all. She opened it and started looking for a verse she knew had to be there. Didn't it say somewhere that the Lord helps those who help themselves?

Old Dog Days

This story features Andy Norton, retired Byerly chief of police and the father of current chief Junior Norton.

"When did you last see him?" Andy asked Payson Smith, but instead of answering, Payson glared at his wife Doreen.

"Around five–thirty, when I got back from Hardee's with dinner," Doreen said. "I cook most nights, but it was so hot that day that I hated to get the kitchen heated up."

Andy nodded understandingly, which he'd done for so many years that it looked pretty convincing. "Five–thirty yesterday evening."

Then Brian piped up with, "It couldn't have been yesterday. We had Kentucky Fried Chicken yesterday, and pizza the night before that. It must have been Wednesday." The boy smirked, pleased with himself for proving his stepmother wrong, not to mention the dig he'd gotten in about her cooking.

"Jesus Christ, Doreen!" Payson exploded. "Are you saying my dog's been missing for three solid days and you didn't even notice?"

"You know I never go out back," she whined, "especially not as hot as it's been. Maybe if we got one of those above-ground pools..." Then, probably realizing that it wasn't a good time to bring that up, she said, "Besides, it's Brian's job to take Wolf his food and water. He's the one who should have figured out he was gone."

Payson turned his glare onto his son, and it was Doreen's turn to smirk.

"Well?" Payson prompted.

"You know I was over at Earl's every day," he said, whining just like his stepmother. "*She* knew that."

"Since when do you tell me where you're going to be?" Doreen shot back.

Andy could tell this was an old argument, so he spoke over them. "Then the last time either of you saw Wolf was Wednesday night, and since Payson was gone until late Friday night, nobody noticed he was gone until this morning. Is that right?"

Doreen and Brian nodded while Payson tried to decide which one deserved to be glared at more.

Andy wouldn't have minded glaring a little himself, but his target wasn't handy. Deputy Mark Pope was probably still at the police station, sitting at a desk he didn't deserve.

If Andy's wife had been there, she'd have told him it was his own fault. It's just that after having been Byerly's chief of police for so long, it was hard to keep from sticking his nose in. He did resist most of the time. After all, he'd trained his daughter Junior as his replacement, and he knew she could handle pretty much anything that came along. Plus she had enough sense to ask for help when she needed it. But Junior was out of town, which left Mark Pope in charge, and that was a horse of a different color.

Mark had been Andy's deputy before he was Junior's, so Andy knew the man wasn't stupid, exactly, but also knew he didn't have the first bit of imagination. Since Andy figured it was nigh onto impossible to solve a tricky case without a little imagination, when he heard about Missy Terhune's murder, it only seemed polite to go down to the station and offer advice.

That's when Andy discovered that Mark had some imagination after all; he imagined that he'd been done wrong when Junior was made police chief over him. Andy didn't know if it was because Mark was a man and Junior was a woman or because Mark was older or what, but Mark sure thought he deserved Junior's job. With her out of town, he was bound and determined to prove it by solving this case on his own.

Not that Mark said that, of course. All he actually said was that he had the situation under control, but the color his face turned after Andy pushed for details meant that the murder was a long way from being solved. When Andy made a couple of suggestions, Mark got mad.

That's when he said there was something Andy could do to help, and Andy said he would, not knowing what Mark had in mind. He'd even let Mark deputize him for the day, the way they did folks who helped with parking at the Walters Mill picnic. Only then had he given Andy the missing dog report and told him to take care of it. To add insult to injury, the dog lived on Butler Street, just two doors down from the murder site.

Still, if Andy had learned one thing in his years as police

chief, it was that people can get just as upset over a missing dog as over a murder, so he had to take it seriously.

"Was Wolf all right when you saw him Wednesday night?" he asked Doreen.

"I guess," she said. "Maybe suffering a little from the heat, but then again, so was I." She wiped her forehead and sighed, probably still thinking about that swimming pool.

"Did you hear anything out of him that night? Or any time after that?"

"Not a peep," she said. "Now that you mention it, that must mean he was gone Wednesday night."

"How do you figure that?"

"Because I *didn't* hear anything. That fool dog barks his head off any time anybody comes near the house, any hour of the day or night."

"He's supposed to bark," Payson said, outraged. "He's a watchdog."

Doreen just sniffed.

"Are y'all sure he didn't get out on his own?" Andy asked. Lord knows, if he only had Doreen and Brian to depend on, he'd get away any way he could.

"Yes, sir," Payson said firmly. "Come take a look at his pen." He led the way out the back door, and Andy noticed that neither Doreen or Brian made a move to leave the air-conditioned house.

What little grass there was in the backyard was brown, making Andy wonder if lawn care was Brian's responsibility, too. Next to the house was a large chicken–wire pen enclosing a patch of dusty red earth and a bone–dry metal water bowl. There was a nice–sized dog house for shade, but Andy kept looking at that water bowl, wondering how long Doreen and Brian had let Wolf go without water during the hottest part of Byerly's long summer.

Payson must have been thinking the same thing because he said, "I don't understand how Brian can treat that dog so bad. Wolf's been part of the family nearly as long as he has. Hell, me and my ex fought more over who was going to get Wolf than we did over who was going to get Brian."

Andy didn't say anything, but he thought that might be the problem right there.

"And Doreen loves dogs," Payson went on. "When my ex wanted to keep Wolf, Doreen fought it tooth and nail. She said she needed him for company while I'm on the road, but we hadn't been married but a month when she found out she's allergic so I had to put him outside. I made him this pen and got the best dog house I could find, but I know the old fellow thought he'd done something wrong."

Though everybody in Byerly knew Doreen had broken up Payson's first marriage, and Andy figured that she'd insisted on keeping the dog to spite the ex–wife, Andy kept what he was thinking to himself as he walked around the pen. There were no holes dug under the fence and no gaps anywhere big enough for anything larger than his daughter Denise's toy poodle to have slipped out. "Wolf is a big dog, isn't he?"

"One of the biggest German shepherds Dr. Josie's ever seen," Payson said proudly. "We took him to her when we first got him, and she could tell that he was going to be a good-sized, strong dog. Smart as a whip, too."

Andy fiddled with the latch on the gate, but not even a canine genius could have opened it by himself. "I don't want to cause any trouble, Payson, but are you sure nobody left the gate open?"

"You heard Doreen—she never comes out here. And Brian would have owned up to it if he had. Somebody must have taken Wolf." He could tell Andy wasn't convinced, because he added, "I called the pound as soon as I found him gone, but they haven't picked up any German shepherds all week. Then I called Dr. Josie, but she didn't know anything about him either. If he'd gotten loose, he'd have ended up at one place or the other."

"Those would be the two places I'd call," Andy said. In fact, he'd have called Dr. Josie first. A lot of people wouldn't take a dog to the pound for fear they'd put it to sleep, but everybody knew Josie Gilpin didn't do that unless it was absolutely necessary. The veterinarian thought dogs and cats had as much right to live as human beings, maybe more so.

Right about then, Andy saw movement a couple of backyards away, behind the late Missy Terhune's house. Mark Pope was walking around, examining the ground as though there were something there to find. He looked over, saw Andy, and gave a mock salute. Andy had such a hard time resisting the kind of salute he wanted to return that all he could manage was a nod.

Payson saw Mark, too. "Wolf must have been gone by Thursday night, or he'd have let folks know there was a stranger nosing around, and Missy might still be alive."

"It doesn't look like it was a stranger," Andy said. "More like Miz Terhune let somebody inside the house and turned her back for a minute. Then whoever it was bludgeoned her with a cast–iron door stop." Andy didn't mind telling Payson this because it was common knowledge already. Besides, Payson was a long–haul trucker who never hit town until late Friday night, so he wasn't a suspect.

"Didn't anybody see him going into the house?"

"Afraid not. I guess she had company coming by at all hours of the day and night, and folks didn't pay much attention." Since her own husband left her, Missy had been cutting quite a swath through the men of Byerly, married and single. It wasn't too hard to imagine that one of them hadn't appreciated sharing and made sure that it wouldn't happen again.

"She was a handsome woman," Payson said, sounding almost regretful. "Of course, it's a shame for that to happen to anybody. And I sure don't like a killing this close to Doreen. If you can't find Wolf, I'm going to have to ask Dr. Josie to help me find a new watchdog."

In most cases, Andy would have told him not to give up so quickly, but he wasn't feeling real hopeful. Still, he owed it to Payson to do the best he could. He turned his back on Mark Pope and said, "Tell you what. I'll see what I can find out and get back to you." He left Payson staring at the empty pen.

Andy had gotten used to having a radio in his squad car to get in touch with people, so a few months after retirement, he'd broken down and gotten a cell phone. He climbed into his car, turned on the air conditioner full blast, and reached for the phone. There were a couple of calls he needed to make that he didn't want Payson to hear.

The thing was, Andy just couldn't see why anybody would have stolen that dog. According to Payson, Wolf was ten years old, and ten-year-old dogs aren't big resale items. While Andy had heard of dognapping rings that sold stolen dogs to laboratories, he'd never known such a ring to operate in Byerly and didn't think a professional would have risked grabbing a barking dog from a pen right next to a house.

What he thought was that somebody had opened the pen, if not Doreen or Brian, then a neighborhood kid. Either way, chances were that the dog had ended up on the road, which meant that he'd most likely been hit by a car.

So Andy called the public works people to find out if they'd picked up any dead dogs. They had disposed of three that week, but no German shepherds. Next he called the dump, but none of the garbage men had brought in a dead dog, either.

Andy still thought Wolf was dead—there were plenty of places a dog's body could be without anybody noticing for a while—but he hated to tell Payson that. Besides, Mark Pope picked that minute to come out of Missy Terhune's house and amble over to Andy's car. Andy reluctantly rolled down his window, and Mark leaned over, looking for all the world as if he was giving Andy a ticket.

"How's the investigation going?" Mark said with a shit-eating grin.

"Pretty routine," Andy said as evenly as he could. "You making any headway in your case?"

Mark shrugged nonchalantly. "Got a few ideas, waiting for some tests to come in. A murder's a lot more complicated than a lost dog, you know."

Andy thought about reminding him how many murders he'd solved, but decided it wasn't worth the effort. "I guess you're right."

Mark seemed disappointed, but kept grinning as he said, "Let me know if you have any problems."

"You bet," was what Andy said, but he was thinking something different as Mark headed for the squad car and screeched away as if he had someplace important to go.

Andy wasn't about to give up after that, so he decided to take the so–called investigation to the next step: questioning possible witnesses. In other words, he talked to Payson's neighbors.

Old Miz Farley, whose house was to the left of Payson's, spent five minutes telling Andy what he should be doing about Missy Terhune's murder before he could explain that he wasn't working on that case. Then he had to listen to ten minutes of complaints about Wolf's barking. According to Miz Farley, she couldn't go outside to water her rose-bushes without Wolf barking loud enough to wake the dead. Unfortunately, Miz Farley couldn't remember the last time she'd heard that barking, and she hadn't seen anybody messing with the dog.

Miz Farley hadn't seen anybody near Missy Terhune's house the night she was killed, either, but that didn't stop her from declaring that it wouldn't have happened if more of Terhune's friends had stayed at home with their wives. Andy couldn't resist asking for details, but Miz Farley insisted that she wasn't one to gossip. He probably could have wheedled more out of her, but instead he reminded himself that it wasn't his case and went to the next house on the street.

Miz Cranford wanted to talk on the porch because her husband Roy was on the night shift at the mill and was asleep inside. She hadn't noticed that Wolf was gone, but now that Andy mentioned it, it had been quiet the last half of the week. Since she worked days at the mill and was home alone at night, sometimes Wolf's barking made her nervous, and it kept Roy up during the day.

Miz Cranford also said she didn't blame the dog for running off because the way Doreen neglected him was a disgrace. She'd started filling his water bowl herself when she watered her lawn. In her opinion, people like that shouldn't have dogs in the first place.

Her indignation made Andy wonder if she'd taken Wolf, but he couldn't figure out how she could be hiding him in her house. Noisy watchdogs didn't turn quiet overnight, not even when given enough water.

The Cranford house was the last on the block, so Andy backtracked to the Titus house on the other side of Payson's, but Mr. Titus couldn't tell him anything. He was so deaf he'd never even noticed Wolf barking. The next house was Missy Terhune's, and the one after that was vacant and for sale.

The vacant place was the last on that side of the street, and though he wasn't sure if he was being thorough or foolish, Andy crossed the street to talk to the people over there. He didn't hear anything other than more complaints about Wolf barking too much and gossip about Missy Terhune's sunbathing in a bikini in her front yard, and he got the distinct impression that nobody was going to miss either of them.

Fortunately, there weren't any houses behind Payson's house, just a patch of woods that blocked the houses from Johnson Road, or Andy would probably have felt obligated to question the folks back there, too. Instead he retreated to his car to try to think of anything he might have missed.

What about the ex–wife? Payson had said they fought over custody of Wolf. Andy couldn't remember her name, so he used the cell phone to call his wife, who always knew such things. It turned out that the ex–wife was on her honeymoon with her new husband, which was why Brian was staying with Payson and Doreen, and Andy couldn't imagine even a devoted dog lover cutting short a trip to Branson to steal Wolf.

Andy was sure he'd taken all the reasonable steps, but Mark Pope's grin was still fresh in his mind. The only thing more humiliating than getting stuck with a trivial case would be messing it up. So he was going to have to do something unreasonable.

He thought about walking through the woods behind Payson's house to see if Wolf had found his way in there and died, and if it hadn't been so hot, he might have done it. Instead, he looked at the sky above the woods. There weren't any birds circling, meaning that there probably wasn't any carrion as big as a dog out there, and if Wolf were still alive, somebody would have heard him barking. So Andy just couldn't make himself go traipsing through the woods when all it was likely to get him was a bunch of ticks.

That dog *had* to be dead on the side of the road somewhere, or at best, injured and nearly dead. Either way, it would be right foolish to drive around looking, so there was no reason for Andy to start driving other than the fact that he didn't want Mark Pope to come back by and find him sitting in his car as if he didn't know what he was doing.

An hour later, he'd driven down every road in Byerly, even those so far away that no ten–year–old dog could have gotten there, especially not with the heat and the condition Wolf must have been in. Andy knew he ought to give up and admit to Mark that he couldn't even find a lost dog anymore. Maybe what they said about old dogs not learning new tricks was true; he and Wolf probably had a lot in common.

As tempted as he was to confess over the phone, he knew Mark would crow that much more if Andy avoided talking to him in person. He pulled into the first driveway he came to, meaning to turn around and head back to the police station, but the driveway turned out to be the one that led to Dr. Josie's place. He decided it couldn't hurt to stop by and ask if anybody had brought Wolf by since Payson called. His wife would have said he was only delaying the inevitable, which he was, but he was thirsty, and maybe Dr. Josie would give him something to drink.

Dr. Josie only saw patients in the morning on Saturdays, so Andy knew the office would already be closed, but since she lived as well as worked at the old farmhouse, he figured she'd be around. When she came outside when he stopped the car, he figured she must have seen him drive up. Or maybe her dogs had let her know he was there—even with the door closed, he could hear all manner of barks and yelps.

"Hey," she said as he got out of the car.

"Hey there. How're you doing?"

Normally he'd have expected a lengthy answer. Dr. Josie wasn't the most talkative person in Byerly, but she was a Southerner. This time her only answer was, "Fine." While

Andy tried to think of what he'd done to offend her, she said, "What can I do for you?"

"I've got some questions about Payson Smith's dog Wolf, if you've got a minute."

Her mouth got tight and she crossed her hands over her chest. "If you think I'm giving that dog back, you've got another think coming, and you're not getting into my house without a court order."

Andy worked hard not to show how taken aback he was. Of course, it did make sense, now that she'd confessed. There wasn't a dog in Byerly that wouldn't come running if Dr. Josie snapped her fingers. "Why'd you do it?" he asked, trying to make it sound like he'd known all along that she was involved.

"If you could have seen that dog, you wouldn't even ask. Skinny as a rail, dehydrated—he'd have been dead by now if I hadn't taken him."

"I don't suppose you had any problem getting him."

"Not a bit. Parked my pickup on Johnson Road and went through the woods to get to Payson's yard." Obviously she didn't share Andy's dislike of ticks, but then again, she couldn't afford to in her line of work. "Poor fellow couldn't hardly walk—he did his best to follow me when I called him, but I had to carry him most of the way to the truck. No creature on earth deserves to be treated like that."

Andy thought for a while. As police chief, could be he'd have felt differently, but as Mark Pope had taken such pains to demonstrate, he wasn't police chief anymore. And even if Payson was fond of the dog, it wasn't fair to Wolf to make him go back to that pen with its empty water bowl.

Dr. Josie was getting nervous. "What are you going to do?"

"Nothing, but this is what *you're* going to do. You're going to call Payson and tell him somebody from out of town hit Wolf with a car this afternoon and brought him here. You did your best, but couldn't save him. Then tell him you buried Wolf already, and you might better put up a marker in case he wants to come see."

"That could work," she said slowly.

"Of course, you're going to have to make sure Payson never sees Wolf again, but unless he gets another dog, he won't have any reason to come out here."

"He better not get another dog," she said ominously.

"Tell him that, too, how bad off the dog was, how maybe he'd have lived if he'd been in better condition. Then suggest that he get a burglar alarm."

She smiled. "Andy, you're my kind of cop. Hey, wait a minute! You're not a cop anymore."

"Nope, I'm retired. Just like Wolf."

She finally invited him in for a Coca–Cola and let him see Wolf. The old dog did look pretty rough, but Dr. Josie thought he'd live another year or two.

It wasn't until Andy was fixing to leave that he thought of something else. "How did you find out about Wolf being without water anyway?"

"A little bird told me."

He just looked at her.

"I mean it. I got an anonymous phone call. Whoever it was must have been talking though a handkerchief, because it sounded funny, but he said Wolf was being neglected. I didn't know if it was a trick or not, but as soon as I saw the old fellow, I knew I had to bring him home with me."

"You don't know who it was?"

She shook her head.

"Would you tell me if you did?"

She smiled again, so Andy just patted Wolf and headed for his car.

The former police chief was feeling mighty pleased with himself. Mark might make a few noises about tracking down whoever it was who'd supposedly hit Wolf, but nothing would come of that. Then he'd make fun because it was only a dog that got hit by a car, but the fact was that Andy had solved his case, when Andy would bet money that Mark wasn't a bit closer to finding Missy Terhune's murderer than he had been that morning.

Imagining how he'd have handled the murder reminded Andy of what Payson had said about it being a shame Wolf hadn't been around the night it happened. Dr. Josie took the dog on Wednesday night, and Terhune was killed on Thursday night. Like Andy told Payson, she must have known her killer because there was no sign of a break–in, and everybody had been assuming that the killer had come to the front door like so many men had. But what if the killer had come to the back door?

Somebody could have parked on Johnson Road just like Dr. Josie had, snuck through the woods, and shown up at Terhune's door without anybody in the neighborhood being the wiser. Of course, Wolf would have barked if he'd still been there, but only a neighbor would have known that.

Then Andy thought about how he could see Terhune's backyard while standing in Payson's. In fact, he could see all the yards down the block; nobody had fences or hedges, and it was hard to tell when one yard ended and the next began. As hot as it had been all week, even at night, nobody had been spending much time outside their air-conditioned houses, so somebody could have walked from one end of the block to the other without ever coming out onto the street and without anybody noticing. Unless, that is, Wolf barked. But Wolf was already gone the night Terhune was killed because somebody had called Dr. Josie. And that somebody was almost certainly a neighbor, because they were the ones who'd have seen how Wolf was suffering.

That's when Andy headed for Butler Street. He was still deputized, so he had a legal right to do what he had in mind. Of course, he didn't have a gun or handcuffs, but he'd rarely used them before retirement, and he thought he could handle one more arrest without them.

Fortunately, she was alone when he rang the bell, and it didn't take much to convince her that she'd be better off if she came willingly. He'd been planning to take her to the police station, but when they came out the door, Mark Pope was standing in front of the Terhune house, talking to Hank Parker, the *Byerly Gazette*'s only full time reporter, and damned if Mark didn't flash that shit–eating grin again when he saw Andy. That's when Andy changed his mind. He escorted Miz Cranford over there and announced that he'd just arrested her for Missy Terhune's murder. Mark was too flabbergasted to speak, but Hank had plenty of questions.

Andy explained how Miz Cranford had found out her husband hadn't spent all day resting for the night shift. Instead, he'd been calling on Missy Terhune. Like many women in her situation, Miz Crawford had blamed the other woman instead of the husband and decided to get rid of her. Getting to Terhune's house without being seen was easy. All she had to do was walk through the backyards. The only problem was Wolf's barking.

Miz Cranford considered poisoning the dog's water, but decided Wolf didn't deserve that, so she called Dr. Josie, knowing she'd rescue him. Like the vet, Miz Cranford was more soft-hearted with dogs than she was with people, because she didn't hesitate for a second when it came to killing Missy Terhune.

Once Andy had realized that Wolf's disappearing the night before the murder was no coincidence, it was easy to figure out that Miz Cranford was the murderer. It had to be a neighbor, because only a neighbor would have known about Wolf's barking, and only the people on the same side of the block as Payson would have been worried about rousing Wolf. That limited the suspects.

There was Mr. Titus, who was deaf and didn't even know Wolf barked, and Miz Farley, but Andy couldn't imagine what motive she could have had. Then there were the Cranfords. Roy Cranford worked at night, so he couldn't have done it, but with him gone and Wolf out of the way, the coast was clear for Miz Cranford.

Mark finally started talking then, trying to make it sound like he'd known all along that the missing dog and the murder were connected, and that Andy had only been following his orders. When he insisted on carrying Miz Cranford to the station in the squad car, lights flashing and siren blaring, Andy knew Mark was going to write up the arrest as his own.

Andy didn't care. He knew the real story, and so did Mark. Besides, Mark hadn't fooled Hank for a minute, and once everybody in Byerly read Hank's article in the *Gazette*, they'd know who had really solved the case.

As he drove back home, Andy decided that even if you can't teach an old dog new tricks, sometimes the old tricks work just as well as they ever did.

Lying-in-the-Road Death

This is the second story featuring Junior Norton. Junior was based on my sister Brenda, and it was always a pleasure to revisit her.

Dan Jackson was as dead a man as I've ever seen, and as long as I'd been Byerly's police chief, that was saying something. As far as I could tell, a heavy set of tires had rolled right over his head, and even though I'd known Dan my whole life, if it hadn't been for the ID in the wallet in his hip pocket, I'd never have known it was him. I decided I'd lost my taste for watermelon for a while.

"You want me to check his other pockets?" my deputy, Belva Tucker, said, but I could tell she wasn't thrilled by the idea.

"Don't bother. Dr. Connelly can take care of it when he gets here."

Belva nodded, relieved.

If I'd been a spiteful woman, I'd have made her do it because of the way she'd held back while I retrieved Dan's wallet, which was one of the most disgusting things I've ever had to do. But since Belva hadn't seen as many bodies as I had, I was willing to cut her a little slack.

"I better talk to Cole." Belva turned to go, too, but I said, "You stay here and keep the critters away from the body." That wasn't spite—it was payback.

Cole Ardmore was still rinsing his mouth out with the bottled water I'd given him when Belva and I arrived. I wasn't sure how many times he'd upchucked his breakfast, but at least he'd kept it away from the body.

"You feel up to talking?" I asked. His panicked 911 call hadn't told me much, just that he'd found a body on Spring-bank Road, and I'd held him off when I arrived until I had a chance to check out the situation myself.

"I'm all right," he said, which he wasn't. "I didn't hit that man, Junior, I swear I didn't."

"I know you didn't, Cole, not unless you did it some-time last night and then waited until daybreak to call me."

He looked confused.

"He's been dead a while," I explained. "Stone cold, and the bugs have already been at him."

He swallowed hard, then gulped down more water.

I knew I was being rough on him, but I also knew he was Dan Jackson's business partner. They ran Littlemill Trucking together, but according to Byerly gossip, the two of them hadn't been getting along. Maybe Cole being the one to find Dan's body was a coincidence, and maybe it wasn't. "You know who it is?" I asked.

"God, how could I? His face..." He shuddered. "I saw the birds first, a whole flock of them all over him. I thought it was a dead skunk or a dog at first, then I got close enough to see." Another swallow of water. "That's when I called you, after I realized it was a person."

"He had ID on him," I said, watching Cole's face as I held up the wallet.

"Jesus, that's Dan's!" He reached for it, but when I pulled it back, he pointed to a worn monogram on the side. "It's got his initials on it. Dan? Dan!" He started toward his dead partner, then abruptly turned back and grabbed hold of a pine tree while he retched again.

Cole was a big man whose usual dusky complexion hinted at some Cherokee or Lumbee in his bloodline. Despite the morning chill, he was sweating profusely. His reaction seemed sincere, but I'd seen quite a few killers cry and go on like that when confronted with their victims. So I watched for any false notes while waiting for the medical examiner.

I got another bottled water out of the squad car for myself, but I'd rather have had a cup of coffee. It was one of those bright fall mornings we have in North Carolina, which would turn to warm or even hot by the afternoon, only to drop down to downright cold come nighttime.

Dr. Connelly showed up a few minutes later, but as he climbed out of the driver's side of his station wagon, a man wearing a Catawba County police uniform got out on the other side. Dr. Connelly was gray-haired, skinny, and what my mother calls spry, meaning that he moves pretty well for a man his age. The other man was right much taller, younger, and with darker hair.

"Hey Junior," Dr. Connelly said. "You didn't drag me away from Shoney's breakfast buffet for a car accident, did you? The county was paying for it, too."

"Sorry about that," I said. "It might turn out to be a car accident, but I want you to take a look anyway. The victim's so messy I'm not sure what happened."

Dr. Connelly cheered up immediately. The man likes his work.

The county mounty stuck his hand out at me. "Deputy Glen Deveron, ma'am. I mean, Chief."

I had a hunch he'd never have forgotten and called a male police chief "sir," and bet myself that he was the kind who gave women wimpy handshakes, fearful of crushing our delicate fingers. I took his hand and confirmed my suspicion. "Junior Norton," I said.

"Junior?" he said, one eyebrow raised.

I could have explained how my father's wish for a son led to my name, but it was my town, so I didn't have to. Instead I said, "What can I do for you, Deputy?"

"Dr. Connelly and I were discussing some cases over breakfast, and I thought I'd tag along. Hope that's not a problem."

"The more the merrier. You want to see the victim? Like I said before, it's a bad one."

"I think I can handle it," he said confidently.

"Suit yourself." Cole was leaning on the hood of his car, trying not to throw up again, which I took as a sign that he wouldn't be running off while the rest of us inspected the remains.

Belva was dutifully standing by, but I could tell the smell was starting to get to her, so after I introduced her to Deveron, I sent her to take Cole's statement. Dr. Connelly was kneeling by the body, happily doing things that I didn't care to think about.

To give Deveron his due, he did take the condition—and the smell—of the body in stride. "You weren't kidding about him being a mess," he said calmly.

"I've seen worse," I said.

"Yeah?"

I gave him a look. "Yeah."

"No offense, it's just that I thought Byerly was a quiet little place. Just the kind of town I'd like to be police chief in once I retire." He held up one hand as if to stop an objection. "Not Byerly itself, mind you. I know you have to be born into your job."

Spiteful or not, I was taking a strong dislike to the man. Byerly may not get as much crime as some places, but that doesn't make being police chief here a walk in the park. And maybe I had had help from my daddy and his daddy when I applied for the job, but I'd done all right with it since then.

Before I could come up with anything worth saying, I noticed Dr. Connelly was watching us. Apparently his morbid curiosity wasn't limited to corpses. "What do you think?" I asked. To make sure he knew what I wanted him to pay attention to, I added, "About the body."

"He's dead."

Deveron snickered, but I just waited.

"Sorry," Dr. Connelly said. "From the size and depth of the tire marks, I'm thinking something big."

"Like an SUV?"

"More like an eighteen-wheeler."

I looked speculatively down the road. "Littlemill Trucking is about half a mile that way. That's where Cole was headed this morning, and I bet Dan was either headed there or away from there when this happened."

"Cole and Dan?" Deveron asked.

"Cole Ardmore, the man who found the body. Dan Jackson, the body."

"How'd you ID him?"

"His wallet."

"It was in his pocket?"

"Where else?" Then I realized what he was getting at. "Yes, I was able to overcome my womanly squeamishness long enough to reach into the dead man's pocket."

"I didn't mean—"

I cut him off, maybe even spitefully, and to Dr. Connelly I said, "Any conclusions?"

"I'd guess hit-and-run, unless you see something I don't." He started to pack up his equipment.

"More a case of what I don't see," I said. "No skid marks, no signs of a vehicle swerving." Both Deveron and Dr. Connelly looked at the unmarked blacktop, and the undisturbed trees on either side of the road. "You'd think there'd be some reaction to hitting a man."

Dr. Connelly scratched his head. "Maybe he didn't realize he'd done it. A man's body wouldn't make much of a bump to an eighteen-wheeler."

"True," I admitted, "but it seems like he'd have noticed when he first hit him."

Then Deveron asked, "Did you know the deceased?"

"Moderately."

"Was he a habitual drinker?"

"I'll say," Dr. Connelly said. "Dan started drinking in high school—I doubt he's even got a liver left."

Deveron nodded sagely. "Then this could be lying-in-the-road death."

The doctor stopped packing and gave a slow whistle. "I've read about that, but I've never seen a case." He leaned closer to the body, not something I'd have wanted to do. "You might be right."

"Would one of you like to clue me in?" I said as patiently as I could.

"Don't be embarrassed about not having heard of it," Deveron said. "I don't suppose you've seen much of it in a small town like Byerly."

I waited for him to get to the point while wishing it were legal to arrest someone for being a sexist snob.

"It was the state medical examiner in Raleigh who did the research into the phenomenon," he said.

"Lawrence Harris," Dr. Connelly put in.

"That's right. He realized an unusual number of intoxicated pedestrians had suffered nighttime collisions on back–country roads like this one."

"What's so unusual about drunks getting hit by cars on dark roads?" I asked

"The fact that most of them were reclining."

"Come again?"

Deveron elaborated, using the same tone as my least-favorite Sunday school teacher. "Harris theorized that as the temperature dropped overnight, men would lie down on comparatively warm blacktop roads, which still retained the day's heat, and go to sleep. They wouldn't wake in time if a car came by, and they'd be next to impossible for the drivers to see. Hence, lying–in–the–road death."

I might have accepted it, even thanked him for the information, if he hadn't flashed such a shit-eating grin afterward. "Is there anything to this?" I asked Dr. Connelly.

"Like I said, I've never seen a case, but Harris's research seems sound enough." He stood up and brushed off his hands. "There's no obvious impact wound like you'd expect to see if a truck struck him. The only injuries are from when he was run over. With the dark clothes he's wearing, it would have been mighty hard to see him."

"He could have been trying to get away from the truck, tripped, and then been hit," I pointed out.

"Maybe," Deveron said, "but I bet when you find the truck driver who did this, he'll tell you he never even saw the man."

"You know, almost every hit-and-run driver I talk to says that."

Before Deveron could answer, the ambulance arrived to take Dan's body away, and Dr. Connelly took charge to make sure everything was done to suit him. I decided to ignore the county mounty's presence and go talk to Belva about Cole. "What'd you get?" I asked her.

"Not much. Cole was on his way to work, saw the deceased in the road, and called us on his cell phone. He wanted to call work and let them know why he was late, but I told him we'd rather he didn't."

"Good."

"Who's the mounty?"

"God's gift to ignorant country police chiefs, or so he thinks. He's already decided this is a case of lying-in-the-road death."

"Say what?"

I explained it to her.

"It sounds reasonable," she said cautiously, and I knew she was wondering what my opinion was.

I couldn't enlighten her because I didn't have an opinion yet. All I knew was that I really wanted to show up Deputy Know-it-All.

"Tell you what," I said. "I'm going to hitch a ride with Cole. You stay here, and after the body is removed, search the area."

"How far do you want me to go?"

"Maybe fifty, a hundred yards. See if you can find out which way Dan came from, whether it was down the road or out of the woods. When you're done, come on down to the warehouse and pick me up."

"Am I looking for anything in particular?"

"Nope. Just bag anything that might come in useful."

"You got it."

Cole was just as glad that I was going to be there to break the news to Dan's wife, Rose. She was a pretty, freckled blonde who worked at Littlemill, too, answering phones and taking orders. Telling a woman she'd just become a widow wasn't my favorite thing to do, but it was part of the job.

Springbank Road dead-ended into the parking lot for Littlemill Trucking, and I saw three other cars parked there.

"Who else is likely to be here?" I asked Cole, hoping Rose had a girlfriend handy to help her through the first shock.

"Just Rose and Keith."

Keith Nevis was the company bookkeeper, though he liked to call himself the chief financial officer. He was skinny and intense looking. "What about the third car?"

"That's Dan's. Rose took his car keys away last night so he wouldn't get hurt." Cole snorted. "I guess he sobered up enough to go find another bottle and get drunk all over again. He had stashes everywhere—it'll probably take a year to find them all."

Cole let us into the warehouse, and led me through the building. I was surprised by how empty and dusty it was, with no trucks in any of the bays.

"Kind of quiet around here today," I said.

Cole snorted again. "It's been kind of quiet for a while now."

"Sorry to hear that. I know times are tough."

"Times are always tough when you've got a partner who only makes it into the office two days out of seven, and when he does come, he screws up the paperwork, forgets to send trucks when he promised, and pisses off most of the drivers so bad they quit. When he's not drinking up the petty cash, that is." He shook his head. "I know I shouldn't be speaking ill of the dead, but Dan... Let's just say that I didn't pick the best partner in the world."

I made a noncommittal noise, while wondering about his and Dan's partnership agreement. Sometimes they're written so that the surviving partner gets the business, or at least the opportunity to buy out the other partner's heirs. Would Cole get Littlemill Trucking now that Dan was gone?

I let Cole precede me into the office. Rose was at her desk, with Keith standing next to her. "It's about time," Rose said as he walked in. "Have you seen Dan? He—" Then she caught sight of me, and her face went white. "Junior? Is it Dan?"

There was no way I could break it to her gently—even trying would only have prolonged the agony. "I'm sorry, Rose, but he's dead. He was hit by a car."

"But I took his keys—his car is still outside."

"He was on foot."

"Sweet Jesus." She buried her head in her hands, and Cole knelt beside her to put his arm around her while she sobbed. Keith shoved a fistful of tissues toward her and then backed off, clearly not sure what else to do.

I knew she'd want to know more, so I waited for the first storm to subside. Sooner than I'd expected, she lifted her head and took a couple of ragged breaths. "What can you tell me, Junior?"

"Not much," I said. "If it's any comfort, it was quick. He didn't suffer."

"Thank God for that."

"It looks as if it happened last night. Cole found him on his way here, and called it in."

"Last night?" she said. "Why wasn't it reported sooner? Where's the driver?"

"I don't know, not yet anyway. If y'all are up to it, I have some questions."

"Of course, whatever you need." She hesitated. "He's not still out there, is he?"

"No, he's been taken care of."

That seemed to comfort her. "What do you want to know, Junior?"

For a murder investigation, I try to conduct separate interviews, but I don't usually bother for an accident. Unfortunately, I didn't know what this case was. I decided to tackle them all at once, both to see how they acted and so they wouldn't have time to talk amongst themselves. "First off, when did y'all last see Dan?"

Keith spoke up. "It was nearly six-thirty, though I normally leave for the day at five-thirty. Unfortunately I needed

Dan's signature on some tax forms, and he didn't get here until nearly six. He'd been drinking."

"Again." Rose sighed.

Keith went on. "I wanted him to sign the form so I could leave, but he and Rose were talking."

"What we were doing was arguing," Rose said. "There's no reason to lie about it, Keith. I imagine we got pretty loud, too."

Keith looked embarrassed. "At any rate, once they were done, I came in to get Dan's signature." He grimaced. "It was sloppy, but recognizable. Afterward, I made photocopies, got the originals ready to mail, and left. That would have been nearly six-thirty."

"What about you, Rose?" I asked.

"I left maybe half an hour after that," she said. "After Keith left, I went back in to talk to Dan, but he'd found another bottle by then and was drinking again. He wouldn't come home with me, and I didn't want him driving in that condition, so I took his car keys and told him to sleep here." She nodded at the vinyl–covered couch along one wall. It looked old, but comfortable, and there was an afghan and pillow, too. I suspected Dan had spent more than one night there.

"He'd nearly passed out by the time I left, and I thought sure he'd sleep through the night. He always had before." She went over and hugged the pillow to her chest. "Why on earth didn't he stay here?" The tears came again, and I had a feeling that this bout was going to last a while.

"Let's finish this outside," I said to Cole and Keith. "I think she needs some time."

Rose nodded and waved us away, and the two men and I went out to the parking lot.

"How about you, Cole?" I asked. "When did you see Dan last?"

"I left around a quarter after seven," he said. "Payson Smith came in from a run late yesterday afternoon, and after he got his paperwork squared away, I drove him into town for dinner. I brought him back out here at eight-thirty or so, but I didn't go back inside and I don't think he did either."

"Why did he come back?"

"To get his rig. He was going to park it at his house over-night and head out first thing this morning."

The timing sounded right. "Do you get many other trucks down this way? Other than your guys?"

"A few," Keith said.

"Not many," Cole said. "But you can't think Payson hit Dan. He'd never have left him like that."

"Maybe he didn't realize he'd hit him." I didn't want to bring up Deveron's theory quite yet. "So you didn't see Dan on the road when you left Payson?"

"No, I didn't go that way."

"I thought Springbank dead-ended here."

"It does, but there's a shortcut into town." We walked a few yards down the road, and Cole pointed out a tiny dirt road I'd forgotten was there. "Springbank takes you out to Highway 321, but going that way cuts the drive in half. Of course, the big rigs have to take the blacktop."

"Would Rose have taken that way last night?" I asked.

"Naturally," Keith said. "I did, too. It's the shortest way, and I wanted to get home."

"Let's get this straight. Last night, Keith went that way, then Rose did, and then Cole and Payson. Later on, Cole brought Payson back, and headed to Byerly on the dirt road while Payson drove out Springbank Road in his truck. Is that right?"

Both men nodded.

"My only question is this. Cole, why were you on Springbank today instead of taking the shortcut?"

"I had to run by the post office this morning, which put me closer to Springbank," he said.

That sounded reasonable. "All right, then. Now I need to talk to Payson. Can y'all get in touch with him, or tell me where to find him?"

Keith went inside to check on the trucker's whereabouts, and ran back a few minutes later. "You're in luck. There was a delay when Payson went to pick up his load, so he's still at the factory in Hickory. I told him to stay put until you get there."

I got the address and radioed Belva to come get me. It wouldn't have taken a Deputy Deveron to detect that she wasn't real happy when she showed up.

"I take it you didn't find anything?" I said as I got into the car.

"Do used condoms count? How about wadded up newspapers or three sneakers, all from different pairs?" She pulled a face. "Nothing but trash, and none of it was fresh."

"It was worth a shot."

She muttered, "Easy for you to say," which I pretended not to hear.

On the way to Hickory, I radioed the police dispatcher there to let them know a couple of out-of-town officers were crossing the border, but I regretted being so polite when I saw the county car parked outside the furniture factory where we were going to meet Payson. Deputy Deveron was sitting in the front seat.

He stepped out when Belva and I did, and said, "Good morning again, Chief. Deputy."

"Morning," I said, not willing to qualify it further. "Who are you tagging along with this time?"

He flashed that irritating grin again. "I heard you on the squawk box and wondered if you were working that lying-in-the-road death."

"I'm working the Jackson case, if that's what you mean."

"I'm telling you, it's a clear case of lying-in-the-road death. I've seen them before."

"Thank you for sharing the depth of your experience, but I have somebody to talk to." I started to walk past him.

"The physical evidence matches—blood traces on the front tires, but no markings on the hood," he said.

I stopped. "What did you say?"

"I said— Oh, don't worry. I didn't touch anything."

"Deputy Deveron, are you saying that you interfered in my case?"

"I just looked."

"Did anybody see you looking at the truck? The driver, for instance?"

"I don't think so."

"You don't *think* so."

"Look, I'm just trying to help." He drew himself up. "I am still in my jurisdiction, which is more than you can say."

I thought about reminding him that I had permission to be there, or pointing out that my daddy had played poker with Hickory's police chief for twenty years, but it just wasn't worth it. Instead I turned my back on the man and said, "Belva, would you get Payson to come out here? I'll be over at his rig."

Deveron at least had the courtesy to stay back at his car while I located the blue-and-white Littlemill truck, and leaned down to examine the tires. It was hard to tell, but I thought I saw blood traces and other smears. And as Deveron had said, I couldn't find anything on the grill or front bumper to indicate a collision.

A few minutes later, Belva brought out Payson Smith, a wiry man in a straw cowboy hat. "Hey, Payson," I said.

"Hey, Junior. Is something wrong?"

"I'm afraid so. You mind telling me where you were yesterday afternoon and evening?"

Payson looked a little worried, but no more than anybody would be when questioned by the police without knowing why, and he gave the same story I'd heard from Cole. When I asked, he confirmed that he'd driven down Springbank the previous night.

"How fast were you going?"

"I don't know. Maybe thirty-five."

I didn't have any idea he'd been going that slow, so I just looked at him.

"Sorry," he said sheepishly. "I was probably going about fifty. I know the road's marked thirty-five, but—"

I held up one hand. "I'm not here to give you a speeding ticket, Payson. I just want to know if you saw anything along Springbank."

"Like what?"

"Like a man's body. Dan Jackson was run over last night."

"Jesus! Is he dead?"

"Oh, yeah. Looks like he was hit by an eighteen-wheeler."

"But I was the only truck— Junior, are you saying I hit him?" His eyes got wide. "I couldn't have. It was dark and I was going fast, but I've been driving a truck for over fifteen years. I couldn't have hit a man and not realized it."

"So you didn't see him?"

"Junior, I'd swear on a stack of Bibles that I did not see anybody on that road last night."

I'd had suspects swear even more drastically than that and still be lying, but I thought Payson was telling the truth. "Let me ask you a question, since you've been driving so long. What if there'd been a man laying in the road last night, maybe wearing dark clothes and not moving. Would you have noticed if you'd hit him?"

He pulled his hat off to scratch his head. "Why would anybody have been laying in the road?"

"Lying in the road, actually," a voice said from behind him. Damned if Deputy Deveron hadn't walked up without my noticing.

I ignored him. "Just suppose he was. Could you have hit him and not realized it?"

Payson gave it some thought. "You know, I think I could have. Even a big man is nothing to a rig like mine. Do you think that's what happened?"

I shrugged. "It's a possibility."

Deveron had the nerve to say, "A good possibility," but shut up when I glared at him.

I said, "If you don't mind, Payson, I'm going to take some pictures of your rig, and Belva is going to scrape some samples off of your tires and the grill for testing."

"Go ahead, I want to know, too." He shook his head.

"Fifteen years without an accident, and now this. And for it to be poor old Dan Jackson."

I patted him on the shoulder and went back to my squad car for the camera and some evidence bags. Deveron was right behind me.

"Classic lying-in-the-road death," he said. "I don't like to say 'I told you so...'"

"Good, because I don't like to hear it." At least I managed to smile when I said it.

Deveron, of course, grinned that grin again.

I halfway expected him to hang around while Belva and I collected evidence off of every one of those eighteen wheels, but apparently he did have some work to do, because he left before we got started. Payson stayed to watch, looking mournful, and he promised not to move the rig or leave town until he heard from me.

After we were done, we drove to Dr. Connelly's office to drop off the samples. I let Belva take them in, but it wasn't for spite—I just didn't want to hear Connelly crow about having found a whole new way for somebody to die.

The rest of the day was business as usual, but around four, Dr. Connelly faxed us the autopsy report and the results of the tests on the samples from Payson's truck. As expected, Dan had died as a result of severe trauma to the head and chest, and his blood alcohol level was several times higher that the legal limit.

That should have been the end of it, but something was niggling at me, and it wasn't just spite because Deveron had figured out the story ahead of me.

I looked over the bits and pieces Belva had gathered together, and something clicked. Before, I'd told Dr. Connelly that I was curious about what I didn't see at the accident scene, meaning the lack of skid marks. But looking at the things Belva had found, I realized there was something else I didn't see, something that sure should have been there.

I called Dr. Connelly just long enough to verify some information from the autopsy report. Then Belva and I went back to Littlemill Trucking to arrest Dan Jackson's killer.

What with the arrest, dealing with lawyers, the paperwork involved, and having to spend the night at the jail to watch my prisoner, it wasn't until the next morning that I remembered that I ought to call Dr. Connelly and let him know what had happened. It turned out he was in the car on his way to meet Deveron for breakfast, since I'd interrupted their meal the day before, and I asked if he'd mind my joining them.

"I thought you didn't like that Deveron character," Belva said when I got off the phone.

"I don't," I said with a grin that I suspected was an awful lot like Deveron's.

The two men were waiting for me at a table at Shoney's, and Dr. Connelly had already poured me a cup of coffee, half of which I downed right way.

"Rough night?" Deveron said.

"A long one, anyway," I allowed. "Guard duty—I arrested a man in the Jackson case."

"The lying-in-the-road death?" Deveron said incredulously. "Don't tell me you arrested that trucker!"

"No, he was telling the truth about not knowing what he'd done because of Jackson lying in the road. Or is that laying in the road? I never could keep those two straight."

I thought about it for a minute. "Now, a person lies down, but lays somebody else down. Isn't that right?"

"What are you talking about?"

"I just want to get my report correct. The fact is, Jackson didn't lie down in the road—somebody laid him down. He was murdered."

"Is that right? Was it Payson?" Dr. Connelly asked.

"Nope, it was Keith Nevis. He told me he was the first to leave work yesterday, and he did drive away, but he didn't go far. He pulled off the road someplace where he couldn't be seen, waited for Rose and Cole to go by, and doubled back to get Dan. He said Dan was so drunk he had to carry him out to his car, which fits in with the elevated blood alcohol level from the autopsy. He drove down Springbank a piece, pulled Dan out of his car, and laid him in the road, knowing that Payson was going to be driving that way later that night. Then he went home, figuring he was safe. If Dan woke up before Payson's truck got him, or if the truck missed him, everybody would assume Dan had wandered off on his own and Dan himself sure as heck wouldn't remember Keith putting him on the road. Which would leave Keith free to try again. Shoot, for all we know, this may not have been his first attempt."

"How can you know the vic didn't walk there himself?" Deveron said, not willing to give up. "Blood alcohol levels can be misleading with habitual drinkers. He might have sobered up enough to walk that far."

"Then why didn't he take the shortcut to town instead of the long way around? And why did he pass out on the road if he was that sober?"

"He was too drunk to find the shortcut because he started drinking again."

"That's possible, because he had bottles hidden all over. But with all the trash Belva collected from around the body, there wasn't one empty whiskey bottle, or beer can, or anything other container for alcohol."

"But—"

"Besides which, Keith has already confessed. Apparently he's been carrying a torch for Rose for years, and he just couldn't stand to see her wasting her life on a drunk. He was probably planning to marry her himself, if she'd have him."

"So no lying-in-the road death after all," Dr. Connelly said, sounding disappointed about not having something new to talk about with other medical examiners.

"There is one thing that might make you feel better," I said as if it had just occurred to me. "You, too, Deputy, since you were so sure you had the case figured out."

"What's that?" Deveron said unenthusiastically.

"Well, Keith was standing on Springbank Road when he told me he went straight home, but it turned out he was lying. So it really was lying-in-the-road death." I smiled at him, then headed for the buffet to get some breakfast.

Maybe I am a spiteful woman after all.

About the Author

Despite her Massachusetts address, Toni L.P. Kelner is a bona fide Southerner, with a double name (Toni Leigh), a slew of relatives scattered throughout North Carolina, and the accent to prove it. Toni is the author of the Laura Fleming mysteries and the "Where are they now?" series, and as Leigh Perry, writes the Family Skeleton mysteries. Toni is also the co-editor of seven urban fantasy anthologies with Charlaine Harris, and has published a number of short stories. She's won an Agatha Award and a RT Book Review Career Achievement Award, and has been nominated multiple times for the Anthony, the Macavity, and the Derringer.

Toni grew up in northern Florida and North Carolina, and currently lives near Boston with her husband, fellow author Stephen P. Kelner, Jr.; their two daughters; two guinea pigs; and an ever-increasing number of books.

You May Also Like...

If this is your first introduction to Laura Fleming and the folks of Byerly, North Carolina, be sure to check out the first book of the Laura Fleming mystery series, *Down Home Murder*!

If you've read all of Laura's adventures, then you may also like *Curse of the Kissing Cousins*, the first novel in Toni L. P. Kelner's "Where Are They Now"? mystery series, featuring savvy celebrity reporter and amateur sleuth Tilda Harper.

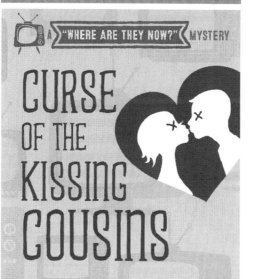

DOWN HOME MURDER

a Laura FLEMING MYSTERY

TONI L. P. KELNER

A "WHERE ARE THEY NOW?" MYSTERY

CURSE OF THE KISSING COUSINS

TONI L.P. KELNER

FOR NEWS ABOUT JABBERWOCKY BOOKS AND AUTHORS

Sign up for our newsletter*: http://eepurl.com/b84tDz
visit our website: awfulagent.com/ebooks
or follow us on twitter: @awfulagent

THANKS FOR READING!

*We will never sell or giveaway your email address, nor use
it for nefarious purposes. Newsletter sent out quarterly.

Printed in Great
Britain
by Amazon

31211990R00154